Call It a Gift

WESTERN LITERATURE SERIES

Call It a Gift

VALERIE HOBBS

University of Nevada Press / Reno & Las Vegas

Valerie Hobbs

Western Literature Series

University of Nevada Press, Reno, Nevada 89557 USA

Copyright © 2005 by Valerie Hobbs

Manufactured in the United States of America

Design by Carrie House

Library of Congress Cataloging-in-Publication Data

Hobbs, Valerie.

Call it a gift / Valerie Hobbs.

p. cm. — (Western literature series)

ISBN 0-87417-612-3 (pbk. : alk. paper)

1. Older people—Fiction. 2. California, Southern—
Fiction. 3. Retirees—Fiction. 4. Widows—Fiction.
I. Title. II. Series.

PS3558.O33665C35   2005

813'.54—dc22   2004017238

The paper used in this book meets the requirements
of American National Standard for Information
Sciences—Permanence of Paper for Printed Library
Materials, ANSI Z.48-1984. Binding materials were
selected for strength and durability.

FIRST PRINTING

14 13 12 11 10 09 08 07 06 05

5 4 3 2 1

For my mother, Alise

Acknowledgments

This book has been fortunate to have many perceptive, intelligent midwives of both genders over the years. Thank you, Myrna, for our walks and talks that guided me so surely in the writing of this story and so many others. A special thanks to all the members of Wheels—James, Mashey, Grace, Judy, Dean, Jenny, Jean—who have nurtured this story in all its forms. And to Frances Foster and Barbara Markowitz, blessings and gratitude for all you have done and continue to do. And to my mom, thank you for never giving up, ever, on anything. And always to Jack, without whom nothing this magical happens.

Call It a Gift

Prologue

Jeronimo drew the paddle through the blue-black water, watching ripples fan out and flatten. The cold air had cleared his head, infused his body with borrowed strength. For the first time in a long while his bones and spine felt limber, purposeful, as if his body had been put together at birth to navigate a canoe.

He looked up and saw the land retreating, grays and browns, a winter's landscape. He thought about how deep the lake was, how cold. And he thought it strange that he hadn't considered until now what would happen if the canoe tipped, hadn't thought about how quickly in the near-freezing water it would all be over. Death had been on his mind for days: her death, then his own. He was no longer afraid of it, or else he'd just grown numb with all the talking, all the thinking about how it would happen and when.

"Far enough, my love?"

Perched in the bow, her hands clutching the gunnels, Emily appeared to have been swallowed by his red-and-black-checkered jacket. Jeronimo could see nothing of her face beneath the knit cap but her gray eyes. It was enough. From the first time he saw her, before he even knew, it had been enough just to be mirrored in those eyes.

"I think you've got the hang of it," she said.

"Just like riding a bike."

Her deep, merry chuckle said she was onto his game. She'd known all along what he was up to. Why hadn't he just confessed when they found the boat at the edge of the lake that he didn't know the first thing about canoes? Instead he'd settled her in the bow with an exaggerated flourish and taken the center seat proprietarily, as if certain all along about what he was doing.

Well, he had gotten the hang of it, enough at least to impress her. She didn't ask to be impressed, never had, and yet out of some outworn creed he didn't even know he knew, he continued to try. It was what men did. But he was nearly exhausted. What strength he had remaining would have to get them back to shore. He lifted the paddle and laid it across his wet knees.

"It's as if we're captured inside a child's snow globe, Mo," she said, gazing up at the white-mottled sky. "Two figures bobbing about in a tiny tin boat for all eternity."

"What a romantic you are, Emily Parsons," he teased.

"Me?" Up went the eyebrows. "I'm not the romantic. Whatever gave you that idea? You're the one. You're the one in love with poetry."

He grinned sheepishly. Such a stupid awful scene he'd made that day in the library over a book, and she'd taken a chance on him anyway. So much life, so much laughter in her eyes. Even now. A child's snow globe. So fanciful, and yet she was right. They had Hart Lake all to themselves, no one around for miles. But when his mind took the next logical step, her analogy chilled him. In whose hands were he and his Emily, the cupped hands of a benevolent God or a God capricious and careless as a child? And if he didn't know after all these years, why tempt fate as they were surely doing now?

But he knew why. It was because it didn't matter anymore.

A flock of geese sailed overhead fanned out in V formation. Jeronimo watched until they were pinpricks in the sky and disappeared. "I can't help thinking of last things," he said. "Like this. Things we'll never do again."

For several minutes she said nothing, then: "Do you suppose it would be the same if we could?" Her eyes gently chided him. "Last things are—"

"Gifts!" he exploded. "I know, I know . . ."

"Mo?"

He ran his hand over the paddle blade where the varnish had worn away. His throat was raw with unsheddable tears.

"I'm not leaving on purpose, you know."

"Oh, Em!" He lunged forward. The paddle clattered to the metal floor. The canoe gave a lurch and he froze, his right hand still reaching for her hand, until the boat was steady again. "I know that. I'm sorry. I just don't know what to do with . . . with endings. I've never been good . . ."

"Is anyone?" She gave his hand a squeeze and released it, holding fast to the gunnels again.

He sighed and sank back into his seat, clutching his paddle. She was right. No one was particularly good when it came to goodbyes. But he was worse than most. He had no words, or the words he stumbled upon were all wrong. Clumsy, inappropriate. Like half the things he did in his life.

"Why couldn't we have met years ago? When we were young. When there was *time*."

Her look softened. "It wouldn't have been the same, my darling. It wouldn't have been nearly as good."

"That's bull crap, Emily. You don't remember, that's all. You've forgotten what it's like to be young and in love."

"Not a bit of it," she said. "It's you who don't remember. The anguish of it all. Of love in the teens and the twenties when one hasn't the self-confidence of . . ." She looked into the water and back at him, her eyes teasing. "Of a fish. I'd have none of it, believe me. What we have, you and I"—her voice softened—"what we've had is love the way it's meant to be."

"The ripeness is all, is it?"

"Exactly."

She rummaged through her fat tapestry bag and pulled out a thermos. He tried to hold the tin cups steady as she poured in the hot coffee. "To adventures," he said, raising his cup and, with it, his spirits. "To Emily Parsons and Jeronimo Martin Smith, two ripe old coots in paradise."

Up went her eyebrows again. "I never said 'old coots.' 'To second and third childhoods' is what I said."

He watched her eyes remembering. Old eyes were so revealing. There was no hiding what you thought or felt when you were old. That surely was the reason the eyes of younger people so often shifted away. It was easier not to know the things that old folks knew, to see the terrible intensity of pain or loss or even of love that old eyes carried.

"We never used the heart-shaped hot tub," she said, both hands wrapped around the warm cup. "What a shame."

"I couldn't even look at it," he cried. "And *you*. You were so far to the other side of that bed, I'm surprised you didn't fall off."

"I thought you wouldn't be interested," she said.

"In you? How could I not be?"

"In sex," she said matter-of-factly. "In older women."

"Well, now, that's true," he teased. "You are an old broad. Seventy-nine to my seventy-seven. Two years is nothing to sneeze at."

"Three," she muttered, mischief in her eyes.

"Three? You said *two*. I've been robbed! I've fallen for a octogenarian!"

The canoe rocked gently on its own now. Wind waves lapped the metal sides, and Jeronimo saw that the shore, toward which the canoe had been drifting, was moving in the opposite direction. "Time to head in," he said with forced calm. He drained his coffee, rinsed the cup in water that numbed his fingers instantly. Taking up the paddle, he saw the weather coming on, dark clouds gathering and lifting as if from cauldrons deep within the earth. There was no keeping the panic from his voice then. "Hold on, Em," he cried. "We're going to have to make a run for it."

He dug the paddle deep and the canoe gave a sickening sideways lurch. "Oh!" she cried, nearly tumbling from her seat. He told himself to settle down. To paddle just as he had before, one single smooth stroke on the left, then another on the right—but the wind came steadily like an intractable moving wall, and he knew he was no match for it. He set his shoulders harder into the paddling, pulling with all he had left against the churning water. Behind Emily's head, past the bare limbs of trees lining the shore, he could see the dark clouds boiling.

1

The day began with a squirt of Preparation H on his toothbrush and went downhill from there. After jamming his big toe against a table leg in the kitchen, Jeronimo cracked the glass coffeepot on the faucet and cut his finger on the glass. Two blocks from the library, he stepped in a great smush of dog crap and had to wash his shoe in the drinking fountain.

Well, what else could he do?

Now Yeats was gone. He ran his bandaged finger over the spine of every book in the poetry section, just in case, as so often happened these days, the book was shelved incorrectly. But it was gone. He would have to request a hold, read some other poet. But he didn't want another poet. Only Yeats could get him through a really bad time, and this one was bad. His forty-seven-year-old son had run away from home. Again. And this time he'd taken the Collected Yeats with him.

At the checkout desk, three middle-aged women stood chattering in a semicircle. As Jeronimo queued up behind them, all three, like schoolgirls in *The Mikado*, turned perfectly painted faces at exactly the same time. Had he said something? Had he been talking to himself again? He felt the blood rise in his neck. His mind was slipping. He knew what they were thinking: Just another old fool.

Well, Santa Barbara was a city full of old fools, people on permanent mental lunch breaks, old codgers hugging the fast lane, creeping along the freeway at forty miles an hour, their minds on distant planets. But he wasn't one of them, not yet. He'd blow his brains out first. If you couldn't keep up, you were supposed to get out of the way.

Unlike the wiry-headed old crone at the head of the line. She'd lost her library card somewhere in that fat, useless bag of hers and had held up the line for who knew how long to search for it. Unconscious. Completely unaware that she was inconveniencing anyone else.

The worn oak floor creaked beneath Jeronimo's feet. He thought about the old days, when he'd have strolled right up to the desk and been greeted by name. He and Miss Dorothea or Miss May (there'd been just the two wonderful old librarians for so many years) would chat about the weather or, better, discuss Jeronimo's discerning choices. "Ah!" Miss May would exclaim. "I'd meant to read that one." Or Miss Dorothea would entreat as he turned to leave, "Do tell me how you find it," as if his opinion had weight and bearing.

Now you had to queue up beside a velvet rope, and all the librarians were young, too young to remember an old patron or validate his wisdom. Everybody was young now. His doctor was forty-three. How much could one know at forty-three? At forty-three, or thereabouts, all Jeronimo knew for sure was that he'd lived his life all wrong, married the wrong woman, settled for stultifying, demeaning work, fathered the wrong sort of son . . .

The wiry-headed woman found her card at last, and the librarian applied a date-stamp. The woman turned, book clutched in her hand. She was a short, spry thing with a firm chin and nice eyes. And that's when Jeronimo saw that the book wasn't her book at all. It was his. It was William Butler Yeats. Collected.

"Aha!" Jeronimo, surprised at finding the book he wanted within reach, erupted in a half cough, half bark and stopped the wiry-headed woman in her tracks. "So!" he cried before he could stop himself. "You have the Yeats."

The woman stood her ground. "Excuse me?" It was the unmistakable voice of nuns and second-grade teachers, the voice of Quiet Resolution. "I've just this minute checked it out. Is there some problem?"

Jeronimo's eyebrows shot up. They were impressive eyebrows, coal black shot with gray, and they grew like tangled weeds. He used them to advantage, changing the minds of people who refused to see things his way. Used his height and his head, too, a dome as bald as the nose cone of a missile. "Problem? Yes, there's a problem. You've got the book I've been looking for."

"I see," she said, edging away as if he were about to attack her, when all he wanted was the book.

"Look," he said, as calmly and reasonably as he could given the shape of his morning, "I *need* that book. Surely there's something else you could read."

The woman smiled, almost mischievously. "Of course there are other books to read, thousands of them. But," she said firmly, no smile now, "I'm up to Y, and so this is the one I'm going to read."

"Damn it, you're being stubborn. Two minutes earlier and I'd have had the book and what difference would it have made to you, anyway?"

He'd wanted to intimidate the little woman, but he hadn't, and so he didn't know quite what to do. He didn't care that he'd been carrying on like a badly behaved seven-year-old or that the *Mikado* women were staring, two in disgust, one in frank amusement. He wanted this woman with the too pleasant face to willingly relinquish what she thought were her rights to William Butler Yeats. He wanted to take the book to the park, settle himself on one of the benches by the pond, and escape his life.

"Here now," the woman said with calm matter-of-factness. "You're making an awful scene over nothing. You may have the book in two weeks, same time, same place. When I return it."

"That's telling him," muttered one of the middle-aged women. "Good for you," said another. Their applause cracked the air like bullets. The wiry-headed woman gave Jeronimo a little cock of her chin and walked off in her sensible old-lady shoes, narrow shoulders squared and set.

Jeronimo threw his arm after the retreating figure, his mouth flapped several times, but his feet stayed stuck in place. What could he do? Charge forward, throw himself in a full-body tackle at those spry little ankles? She'd have probably survived all right, while he with his bum back would have been hauled off to the emergency ward. Worse yet, off to one of those mausoleums where they stored broken old people until they did the world a favor and croaked.

The librarian had just said something. To him, but what was it? He watched her reach toward him and, with the bland insensitivity of the very young, pat his hand. Jeronimo wanted to bite her arm. His neck felt warm, prickly. Nothing seemed to be happening in the Santa Barbara Public Library but this little . . . *scene*, and he was at the center of it. In fact, everyone was behaving as if he had caused it. Well, to hell with them.

He turned away at last, muttering some half apology/half explanation thing, but no one was listening. They had gone back to what they'd come for. Nothing else mattered. No one else mattered. That's what kind of world it was now. No one gave a damn.

2

In the two weeks that had passed since the "little library inci-
dent," as he'd come to think of it, Jeronimo had posted himself
every morning on the library steps. He'd started the very day after
the woman took his book—just in case she found Yeats boring
or trivial (as he suspected she would) and decided to return it
early.

Just why he was doing this wasn't absolutely clear to him. He
could have bought another Yeats, a paperback, to read until Todd
returned his copy. If he ever did. Instead, he found himself hanging
around listening for the telephone to ring. He knew Todd wouldn't
call. If anything, he was even more stubborn than his father. The
silence in the house was deafening, and nothing could alleviate it.

Not the television, not Jack Daniel's. Maybe not even Yeats, though he held out some hope.

Who was to say she'd show up today just because the book was due? She could be the type who accumulated library fines. The careless type. Already he was losing respect for her.

"Have you been here all this time?" She wore blue jeans and sunglasses with oversized white frames, and Jeronimo wouldn't have recognized her had it not been for her wiry head.

He unfolded himself and stood, as steadily as he could given the cramp in his back. She was two steps above him when their eyes met, or rather his eyes and her frames. "No, I haven't been here all this time. You think I'm some kind of nutcase?"

Off came the sunglasses. She started to say something, then changed her mind. Sharp gray eyes regarded him with suspicion — or perhaps genuine dislike. Jeronimo couldn't tell which. Easily offended, he thought. The sulky type.

"Well, the book is yours," she snapped. "I'll just drop it off at the desk and you can check it right out. Though for the life of me . . ." She wandered off in the direction of the circulation desk.

"What?" Jeronimo stayed in her tracks. The worn wooden floors creaked beneath her sensible little shoes, his steel-toed working boots. "For the life of you, what?" The library had that cold, dusty morning smell he loved.

She turned. "What did you say?"

"For the life of you, what? For the life of you, you don't know why I wanted this book? Well, why did you want it?"

Emily laid the thick green book on the counter and glared up at Jeronimo. "What is your name, anyway?" she said in that same impatient tone. "If we're going to have a conversation, we'll have to introduce ourselves. My name is Emily. Emily Parsons."

"Jeronimo," he said. "With a J. Jeronimo Smith."

Emily Parsons looked puzzled, as did most people to whom he introduced himself.

"My old man couldn't spell," he said. He loved having to explain his name. It burnished him with a kind of Old West patina, connected him to less civilized, more exciting times. But he could see he had not impressed this straightforward stick of a woman, and so he changed his tack. "I'll tell you why I wanted the book," he offered as if she'd asked, and hoped he hadn't offended her again. "I mean, if you really want to know. If you've got the time." He felt like a ninny, a child standing cap in hand before his teacher after school.

He watched her hesitate, told himself he didn't care one way or the other. But he did, he did care. For some reason, some stupid reason, this odd little woman mattered to him.

"As it happens I do have some time this morning, a little. My daughter is—." She frowned. "Well, I'm free for a bit if you are. I'll buy us a coffee, shall I?"

She had become perky, almost flirtatious, which of course couldn't be. Elderly ladies didn't flirt, at least not the respectable ones. And they never flirted with him. Still, the change in her attitude put spring into his backbone. He offered his arm, an old-fashioned kind of thing but appropriate, wasn't it? Given their age.

And she took it, took it so beautifully, with a winsome modesty you never found in women anymore, eyes just a little downcast and a sweet, deferential smile.

They sat at an outdoor table, under a canopy of pepper trees, surrounded by juvenile delinquents with multicolored striped hair and nose rings. A breastless young woman with a painted dragon inching over her right shoulder took their order.

"I don't care for tattoos on young women," Emily said when the girl had gone. "Do you? I know it's old-fashioned of me. Times change and all that."

"Vulgar!" Jeronimo spouted. "Positively obscene. A mutilation."

He waved away the smoke that drifted straight at him from a nearby table.

"Oh, it's not that bad," she said. "It's their way. The young people's way of . . . of making a statement. We can't condemn them for trying to be a little different. Shall we sit inside? Is the smoke bothering you?"

"Well, they ought to make their statements somewhere else," Jeronimo cried. "Look at them! Ten o'clock in the morning. On a weekday and what are they doing? Working? Not on your life! Going to college? Hardly. They haven't an intact brain between them. No, the smoke's not bothering me."

Conscious at last of the rising volume of his voice, Jeronimo cleared his throat, cleared it again, as if clearing his throat would clear the air.

She regarded him for a moment, gray eyes flashing. "Do you always, Jeronimo Smith, judge a book by its cover?"

She'd caught him spouting. He hadn't intended to spout. Why couldn't he just carry on a normal, decent conversation? They were supposed to be discussing Yeats. Jeronimo had intended to be his better self, but he hadn't been at all.

The waitress returned with their decaf. Jeronimo tore open three packets of sugar and dumped them into his cup, stirring it violently with the plastic stick provided in place of a decent spoon. In an attempt to normalize the conversation, such as it was, Emily found herself babbling—facts about the family, Alison's job, the children's ages.

She watched the strange way Jeronimo gathered together the three packets of sugar, squaring them just so before tearing them open, and began to wonder why she'd walked off with a stranger who could very well turn out to be a lunatic, even dangerous. What she'd had in mind for her little time away was some shopping. For a hat. Or something. She didn't know why a hat. She never bought hats. It just seemed the thing to do on a bright autumn day. One was supposed to protect oneself from the sun, which was now to be regarded as the enemy. There were great holes in the sky for which she, a faulty human being, was personally responsible. Perhaps she would buy one of those revived Victorian things with paper posies glued to the brim. Or, more likely, she would buy something for her grandchildren. Something to hold their interest for more than ten minutes, if such a thing existed. Shopping bored her actually, but what else could one do in an hour? "I haven't as much time for reading these days," she said, "so I've been working through the poets. It goes faster, don't you think? Yeats is the last one on my list."

"What list?" She came out of left field faster than he could catch the ball.

"My list," she said matter-of-factly. "I began with Auden and now I'm finished. Unless there's a Z."

Jeronimo's eyebrows shot up. "You've read every poet in the alphabet?"

"Well, the major ones. Couldn't find a Q, though, or an X." She paused and studied him for a moment. "And you? Why did you want the book?"

Her question stopped him cold. How could he tell this woman he hardly knew why Yeats was so important to him? She'd see at once how woefully rough and uneducated he really was, despite his decades of reading. What would he tell her when she asked, inevitably, what he'd done with his life? Would he tell her the truth? He'd been a janitor. Well, he'd owned his own janitorial service once. That was something. It made a living. But she came from money, he could tell. From nannies and good private schools. She would never be able to understand the shame of a misspent life.

"It's a long story," he said. "Not worth the telling."

He sipped his decaf, thinking to change the subject. But to what? It had been too long since he'd had any kind of conversation with a woman. He didn't know the moves anymore.

"But that's why we're here," she protested. "You said you'd tell me why you wanted the book so badly, and I offered to buy the coffee."

Her eyes were so inviting, her manner so kind, that he found himself telling the story about Abe Fortnum, who, decades before, had taken a twenty-year-old janitor under his wing, perhaps for the curiosity he'd recognized in a young man's eyes. Jeronimo had come upon the professor late one evening in his book-clogged, smoke-filled office. Abe had thought Jeronimo was one of the students—the buckets and mops were in the hall—and welcomed him inside. Jeronimo hadn't wanted to dispel the professor's illusion, so he'd asked a few what he hoped were halfway intelligent questions about the books. Yeats had caught his eye (he'd said Yeets and the professor had not corrected him—not then).

Abe had awakened—no, *created*—in Jeronimo a whole new being. He'd begun to devour books, to people his lonely world with a host of characters he could have hailed on the street by name if he'd ever run into them. Mrs. Micawber, Elizabeth Bennett, Kurtz and Marlowe. By then he'd grown all too accustomed to living without people, or at least without anyone who cared very much about him. It seemed then that it would always be that way, though there'd been various caretakers after his mother died; foster homes—some beneficent, some brutalizing; stints in juvenile hall, never for long, never for offenses too great. But until Abraham Fortnum no one had bothered to see beneath the tough exterior Jeronimo wore to protect the unformed man inside. No one had recognized his intelligence. No one but Abraham Fortnum.

"I'd have given up the book gladly, had I known," she said softly.

Throughout his telling of the story, her eyes had never left his face. She had not, despite the glare, put on the hideous white sunglasses, for which Jeronimo was grateful. He had more than once refused to converse with people unless they first removed their sunglasses. It was rude, after all. A way to hide what they were really thinking so they could get the best of you.

And, he had to admit, her eyes had drawn him from the first. When she looked at him, she, well, really *looked*. When she listened, she *listened*. He wasn't used to that kind of thing.

"He's lovely in French," she said. "More . . . I don't know, lyrical."

"Yeats?" Up went Jeronimo's eyebrows. "You've read Yeats in French?"

"Well, yes. In school, just a few of his poems. Do you speak French?"

Jeronimo's knees knocked the table, rattling the cups in their saucers. His legs were too long. He couldn't fit them under these ridiculous patio tables. "Of course I speak French." The coffee that had spilled into Jeronimo's saucer demanded immediate attention. He mopped the saucer several times until it was dry, avoiding Emily's eyes.

"You went off without the book you wanted so badly, you know."

She was right. He'd left the book where she'd set it on the counter. After all that. More slippage.

"Actually, I'd planned on buying a paperback," he said, regaining his bearings. "I'm taking off soon. Packing light. Won't need my hardcovers."

"Oh?"

"Selling the farm. Lighting out. Heading up to Montana. You

been up that way?" He didn't think she had. Didn't seem the type. "They call it Big Sky Country and when you're there, you know why. It's like you can really feel the earth is curved under your feet and there's this . . . sky! . . . this blue, I don't know, the bluest blue sky." He stopped, embarrassed, his arms spread wide.

"Sounds heavenly," she said, and blushed. "That was a joke of sorts, wasn't it?"

"What? Oh. Yeah, yeah . . ."

There seemed nothing then to say. The waitress came with their check.

"Well, I suppose I'd better be on my way," she said, reaching for her bag.

"I'll get this," Jeronimo said. He picked up the check, holding it at arm's length to read the total.

"It's my treat," she said.

"I've got it," he said, tugging his leather change purse from his pocket.

Emily reached over and neatly plucked the check from his fingers. Jeronimo tried to snatch it from her the way he'd wanted to snatch the book. But she held on. The check tore in two.

"Why are you so stubborn?" Jeronimo cried, leaping to his feet, knocking the table sideways. He made a futile grab for it as it crashed. His cup broke in two, hers clattered across the bricks. The table lay on its side in a pool of milk and sugar. Emily remained in her chair, looking on in disbelief.

"Hurricane Jeronimo," she said, almost to herself.

"What?" He had righted the table but didn't seem to know what to do about all the rest.

"They should name a hurricane for you," she said.

"Is that another of your little jokes?"

"I suppose," she said, kneeling to gather the pieces of a saucer.

She walked off with the broken china and torn check while he stood watching. Despite the racket they'd made, no one had paid much attention — or appeared not to have. Not that he gave a damn what anybody under the age of thirty thought about anything.

Anybody over the age of thirty, for that matter.

Well, he cared what she thought. Didn't want to, but there it was. He'd intended to be charming. But that was only, he reminded himself, in case she decided to renew the book. He'd been prepared to charm it away from her. What he hadn't intended was to make another scene, or to care so deeply about what the devil she thought of him. Now she would believe that he was in the habit of making scenes all the time. And he wasn't. Was he? And why did he care what she thought, anyway?

"So," she said when she returned, extending her hand. "It was nice to meet you." They stood in the filtered shade of a pepper tree. Leaf shadows swam across Emily Parson's face like a school of anchovies.

"Where are you going?" Jeronimo demanded. "I'm not doing anything much. I could walk you." Leaves tickled the dome of his head. He swatted them away.

"Oh, no," she said. "Don't bother. I'm just going to do a little shopping." She looked up at him, shielding her eyes from the sun with her curved hand. "Yeats is better in English, isn't he? I don't know why I brought up the French."

"Of course. Yes, of course. He's wonderful in his own language. We all are."

We all are? What was he saying?

"Good-bye, then." She gave him a too bright smile and a little wave and headed off down the street.

He began to follow but stopped after a few yards. She hadn't wanted him bumbling along after her. Well, he had things to do, too. Didn't he?

But where did she live? He had to know that. Had to confirm his suspicions. He was sure he knew her type, though everything she said seemed to run counter to his picture of wealthy, self-indulgent, bridge-playing widowhood (and how did he know she didn't have a husband waiting in some fancy turn-of-the-century estate?). He hurried after her, keeping people between them. She went into the new bookstore, one of a chain that Jeronimo refused to patronize. While he waited, he attacked a flyer hung on the door with his blue marking pen, adding an m to community, and changing the e to a in effect. She came out at last, carrying a small green bag, looked to the left, then the right. She didn't seem to know which way to go. Disoriented. She had a funny way of being sharp as a good cheddar, but then something would come over her. Only she didn't seem to let it throw her as it did him.

Like a detective he kept a good eye on her, skulking along as she went into and came out of two more stores carrying the same small green bag. He felt as if were she to turn she would look right through him. He became bolder. On Laguna Street he was not half a block behind. When she stopped to unlatch the gate of a two-story bungalow, number 467, he ducked behind a jacaranda tree and remained there until he heard the front door close.

The house seemed to float unsubstantially within a sea of overgrown grass. His hands itched to get hold of his new mower and bring that grass down. Lawns to the left and right resembled his own neatly trimmed yard, and for a moment he felt embarrassed for Emily Parsons. A woman her size could never tackle a yard like this. It would take every bit of power in a mower like his 40 hp BMX 2000.

He watched from behind the jacaranda until it became clear there was no use standing there. He felt restless, eager for something he didn't know the name of. He wasn't hungry, or tired. In fact, he felt better than he'd felt in days. What he needed was to *do* something.

Stopping at Chaucer's on his way home, Jeronimo found a halfway reasonably priced paperback of Yeats's poems. Not the Collected Yeats, but that would have cost him a bundle. He took it to the counter, but before the clerk could reach for it, Jeronimo abruptly turned and wandered the aisles in search of the French Literature section. He figured that if he laid the books side by side, he'd be able, more or less, to read the Yeats in French.

So there, Miss Emily Parsons, he said. *Aloud?* He swiveled his head from side to side but found himself alone in the aisle. Such were his small blessings.

For the next three days he could think of nothing but her. What was it with him? He wasn't even angry with Todd anymore. Well, except in all the ways he would always be angry with Todd.

Why hadn't he asked for her telephone number? That's what you did if you wanted to see someone again. All he had was her address and the name of the real estate office where her daughter worked.

And did he really want to date a woman whose daughter was a *Realtor?*

3

"You said you'd be gone half an hour." Alison sailed past Emily, arm flailing for the jacket sleeve of her yellow Armani. "How long does it take to sign up for a class? You *knew* I had this appointment."

Sign up for a class? Had she really said that? Why hadn't she told her daughter the truth? That she'd gone on a date. Watching Alison gather her papers, Emily was reluctant to shed the little wings of excitement that had floated her home from the art museum.

Though it hadn't all been exciting, or even fun.

He'd called her. That had been exciting. He'd had to find her phone number after all, which meant learning Alison's last name that he could only have gotten by calling the Century 21 office, the only detail she could remember giving him. Which meant he'd gone to some trouble. Which meant he was interested.

They'd arranged to meet at the art museum. There was a special exhibition of Remington sculptures, he'd said on the phone. Did she like that "sort of thing"? Of course she did. Only after hanging up did she remember who Remington was.

The mistake they made, she supposed, was going through the Rothkos on the way to the Remingtons. Jeronimo, who'd been striding ahead, came to a sudden dead stop in front of a canvas that, as far as Emily could see, was black. "Art!" he'd cried. "They call that art!" Then he'd gone on for several minutes berating the artist, the museum, the world of modern art in general, art patrons, art critics, even art galleries. At last he turned to the guard at the door, whose expression had never lost its bland facade. "You don't have to worry about this stuff," he scoffed, flapping his long arm at the priceless collection. "Nobody's going to steal this. This guy's no Monet, let me tell you."

They'd lingered long enough over the Remingtons to calm him down. "Now that," he'd said, staring down at yet another bronze horse, this one sans rider, "is art."

Afterward they'd gone to the same café. That was when he'd told her the remarkable story about Yellowstone, about the horseback trip with his father and about the bison dying in the snow. She'd been moved nearly to tears. What she'd guessed about him was beginning to reveal itself. There was more to him than met the eye.

He'd walked her home. At the gate, after staring for some time at the grass—belligerently, she thought—he said he'd like to see her again. And was that all right?

Indeed it was.

Now as she watched her daughter stop and peer myopically into the hall mirror, smudge her glistening orange lips together and jab her fingers into thick auburn curls, as disappointing as everything else in her life, as her mother, Emily felt her time with Jeronimo evaporate.

Emily considered answering Alison's question, but it wasn't really a question and Alison wouldn't have listened anyway. What did she know about time, real time? Time that stretched so long and stretched you with it until you thought a day might never end. Alison never had a moment to spare. Time was money. Time was another listing. Time was that house at the very top of West Camino Cielo that no one could sell but that she would sell.

If Alison hadn't been so confoundedly single-minded she'd have looked out the window five minutes ago and spied her mother with a man. What would she have said to that?

"There's some chicken you can pull out and defrost. If I'm not home go ahead and eat. Throw some of that white sauce on it, you know the stuff . . . God! I can't believe what's happened to the time! I've been on the telephone all morning." She leaned forward to brush cheeks with Emily. "I'm sorry, Mother. You know how I hate leaving you with everything." She rummaged in the depths of her black leather bag for her key ring. "Make sure Sam does her homework before you let her out of your sight. TC has soccer practice till five."

Emily watched the yellow flash disappear into the bowels of the minivan with its dented sliding door that would no longer open. She watched her daughter drive away. So fixed, so focused. She supposed it was just the quality one had to have in the competitive world of real estate. She closed the front door and went, as if on automatic pilot, into the living room. On the coffee table were plates left over from the previous evening's dinner, crusted with cheese sauce and stuck dry noodles. The green plaid couch, a sorry thing, was littered with newspaper, sweaters and socks, cat hair. She picked up two of the dirty plates and headed for the kitchen.

"Nana!" The front door slammed. "Nana! Where are you?" Samantha burst into the kitchen, her pale blond hair in tangles.

"I'm right here, Sam. You don't have to yell."

Samantha threw open the refrigerator, stood on her tiptoes to grab a can of root beer, and slammed the door with her foot. "We're going to play Barbies," she announced breathlessly. The can popped and fizzed, brown foam dripped down her fingers onto the floor.

"We?"

"Me and *Carrie*," said Samantha impatiently, as if her grandmother was trying her best not to be smart.

"Homework first, Sam. You know the rules."

"Nana! Carrie's *waiting*." Sam's pale, freckle-strewn face began to redden.

"And she'll wait until you've finished your homework."

Emily ran water into the dishpan, squeezed the soap in. The dishwasher would not be able to clean plates as coated as these.

"I can't do my homework now. Carrie's *waiting*. We're playing *Barbies*. It's rude to keep people waiting."

Samantha stood in the familiar pose of her mother, fists on what would someday be her hips. Three mismatched barrettes had been stuck at random into her hair. On her small round face, bright pink spots had erupted like a rash.

"Now that's my thoughtful child," Emily said brightly. "We don't want to be rude, do we? Telephone Carrie right now. Tell her you'll meet her the minute you finish your math."

Outwitted, Samantha stomped the heel of her Nike against the kitchen floor in frustration. "I can't do it!"

"You can't do what?" She turned to her recalcitrant grandchild. She was tired of Samantha's tantrums, weary of playing bad cop to Alison's good cop. After a day of battling the children into various attitudes of compliance, she would stand helplessly by as Alison undid all her best work by nightfall. "You can't call Carrie or you can't do your math?"

TC sailed through the kitchen on his Death's Head skateboard. "She can't do math!" he hollered. "She's stupid. *Estupido.*"

"Outside with that skateboard, Thomas." She heard the skateboard clip a baseboard in the dining room. "Do you hear me? Outside."

TC sailed back through the kitchen. The back screen slammed. The skateboard went banging down the back steps. Emily's hand went to her forehead as if to take the temperature of her tolerance.

"I'll get you some aspirin," Sam offered in her most syrupy voice. "Then I can go to Carrie's, okay?"

"Not okay," Emily muttered. "Homework. Now. At the table where I can watch you. This minute, Sam."

"You're *mean*," Sam cried. "You're the meanest grandmother in the whole world, and I hate you!"

She ran down the hall to her room and slammed the door behind her. They all slammed doors in this family. They said all the worst things with doors, and it was wearing Emily down.

A year and four months she'd been here. Sixteen months on the way to forever. Fitting the last of the dishes into the dishwasher, she knew with a sickening certainty that her coming here had been a mistake.

The telephone rang. Emily sighed and dried her hands. It was Dr. Mott's receptionist. Was Emily available on Thursday?

"That soon?" Emily said. No reply from the receptionist. Emily sensed what that meant. "Well, yes, I suppose I can come in on Thursday. In the morning. It will have to be in the morning. I have the children."

"Thursday at ten? Doctor said the sooner you start treatment—"

"Ten will be fine," she said. She replaced the receiver, staring at her hand, which looked, for some inexplicable reason, like someone else's hand, someone she didn't know or knew in a previous life. "So," she said to the knocking of her heart. "So."

Treatment. She'd been told about the treatment that wasn't really treatment. There'd be medication, that was all. For the "discomfort."

From the refrigerator, she extracted a sweating package of chicken parts and laid it on the counter. She was strangely calm, separated from herself, as if she'd answered someone else's telephone call, as if she were Kimberly, Dr. Mott's receptionist, a young woman bland as applesauce who could change people's lives in an instant and then go on with her own, unstirred.

From Samantha's room came the sound of small feet beating an angry tattoo against the wall.

4

Emily checked the cupboard for rice and, finding none, went in search of boxed potatoes. It was strange how a body could go on. Well, she had known, hadn't she? Why the surprise? She'd been told the odds.

Ten past four. Ignoring Samantha's wall beating, Emily went into the living room. She sat carefully on the edge of the couch amid the rubble, as if she were somehow lighter, as if she had lost between the ringing of the telephone and this present dark moment some essential substance.

The living room was gray, lifeless, the blinds pinched closed from the night before. She laid a hand against her chest to still the anxious beating of her heart. If she could only cry, beat her feet against the wall. But that was not allowed. Only the young had a right to be indignant in the face of death. The old were expected not to make a fuss. Eskimo grandmothers deposited on ice floes were left to fend for themselves with sightless eyes, knotted useless fingers, teeth that could no longer work the skins or chew their food. She should be grateful.

Or she should have kept the house in Pittsburgh. Her little parlor with its Wedgwood blue love seat, the light that poured a daily benediction through every polished windowpane. But Alison had needed her. Needed someone, and her mother, a recent widow, seemed the obvious choice. California would be so good for her arthritis, Alison promised. And it was. Emily's fingers were now nearly free of pain and completely capable of caring for her two demanding grandchildren. What luck.

Alison knew nothing about this latest thing, this "growth." Funny how many ways the word *cancer* could be avoided. Emily thought there must be an unwritten rule about it at the clinic. There was a "problem," the doctor had said, a "shadow on the films." Dr. Mott was a young man with a shiny round face, an extra chin, and blank brown eyes. His manner was so apologetic, whether for his own youth and robust good health or for the fact that his machines had found the thing that would end her life, that Emily's alarm was momentarily derailed. She skimmed the various diplomas displayed in handsome frames on the wall behind his head. She wondered where Wayne State was. She wondered if Wayne State had a class titled "Benevolent Use and Practice of the Modern Euphemism." Then her body had grown cold and she'd begun to shake at her core. She shook violently through something he called "treatment modalities." Surgery was "not recommended" in her case, he said, frowning at the notes scribbled on her chart.

"Not recommended?"

He blinked several times. "It wouldn't be . . . feasible," he said.

"You mean it's too late."

"It's not recommended," he said, a pleading note having crept into his voice, as if he were a teacher or parent coaching her to learn some academic formula she'd just as soon not know.

She'd left the clinic in a strangely elevated state. The world vibrated with an intensity she'd never before noticed. Colors were deeper, brighter, the sky an ardent blue. Palm fronds shimmered gold and green. She had to look away from a crimson waterfall of bougainvillea crashing down the front of the clinic. People wore silvery auras around their heads. Not just some of the people—all of them.

Shock, she supposed it was.

The telephone rang Emily back into the present. She got up and went into the kitchen, surprised to see Sam's math book open on the table, a bright-eyed Sam on the phone. "Mommy says she'll try to be home for dinner," Sam said, holding the receiver across her narrow chest.

"Tell her we'll slay the fatted calf," Emily said dryly.

"Nana says—"

"Never mind, darling." Emily reached for the receiver. "Alison, we're out of rice and potatoes. There's nothing remotely resembling a vegetable. The children and I are having chicken and canned pork and beans. You're welcome to join us, of course." She listened some more. She heard herself sigh, as she too often did these days. "Oh, do. Do, by all means. Pork and beans isn't one of my favorites either." She hung up the phone.

"Nana?" Emily was not at all surprised at Sam's sudden change of mood. An easily bored child, she often had the good grace to grow weary of her own awfulness.

Emily pulled out a chair and sat beside Sam. "Do you need some help?"

"Uhn-uh. This is baby stuff."

"Then what, darling?"

"Nana," said Sam very seriously, her forehead scrunched in thought. "You know, sometimes you just have to do things. Even if nobody wants you to. Do you know that?"

Emily quickly scanned the myriad things Sam might have in mind. "What kinds of things, Sam?"

Sam frowned. "I dunno," she said. "Things. Like . . . playing Barbies." Her small round face was squinched in thought.

"Right after school, you mean."

"Uh-huh."

"Instead of doing homework."

A power lawn mower snarled into life. Bob Layton next door, she decided, manicuring his already perfect lawn. What must he think of their sorry yard? The grass came nearly to Sam's waist, which of course Sam thought was great.

"I'm sorry I said you were mean," Sam said.

"Thank you, darling. I am mean sometimes, you know. I'd like to think it's for your own good, but sometimes I just get tired and run out of patience."

The Laytons didn't have a power lawn mower. Bob Layton mowed every square foot of his yard with an old-fashioned push mower. It kept him young, he said. Emily glanced out the window toward the Laytons' but saw no one. The mower droned on.

Sam studied her grandmother's face. "Are you old, Nana?"

"What do you think, Sam?"

Sam plunked her cheek on her fist and peered up at her grandmother through the loose strands of her hair. She looked troubled but resolute to convey her painful dose of truth. "I think you're pretty old," she said.

"I'll tell you a secret," Emily said. "In here"—she touched her chest—"I'm not old at all. I'm, well, about your mother's age. About forty-six."

"Don't be silly, Nana."

"It's true, darling. People age on the outside, but inside, why, they can be any age at all. Different ages on different days. Can you imagine?"

But Sam had reached the end of her interest in gerontology. "You didn't make me my cookies and milk, Nana," she said. "And I'm almost finished with my homework."

The sound of the mower grew louder. A shadow fell across the table as a figure passed the kitchen window. The sound of the mower retreated with it.

"Who's that, Sam?"

Sam shrugged. "I dunno."

"Are you sure? Did your mother hire someone to cut the lawn?"

She got up and went to the back door, but the mower had gone to the front. The back lawn had been stripped to the skin. It lay in perfectly straight dead brown and greenish-yellow stripes. Emily could imagine whatever had been living in all that grass running for cover, grabbing whatever could be grabbed and lighting out for new territory. The Laytons' fat tabby gazing from the adjoining yard looked frankly astonished.

Emily went through the house and out onto the front porch. Afterward she told herself she should have known. But that was silly. How could she possibly have known? And yet it seemed something only Jeronimo Martin Smith would think to do. His back was to her as he guided the big machine toward the Laytons'. Sweat sealed the khaki workshirt to the long narrow back. She noticed again that his shoulders were very broad, like Gary Cooper's. In earlier years, when she was young and stupidly romantic, that in itself would have been enough to propel her straight across the remaining grass and into his arms. Now, she was simply annoyed. Who in God's name did this man think he was?

He turned the mower at the fence, and she expected him to see her standing there on the porch. But his eyes were on his own hands or perhaps on the grass just ahead of the mower, and his mind was somewhere else entirely. He looked angry or sad, she couldn't tell which—perhaps simply determined. He looked up finally when he reached the narrow walkway. His eyebrows lifted. He switched off the motor. The sounds of the world came back, a plane droning overhead, traffic on the cross street, crows in the eucalyptus.

"What are you doing, Jeronimo?" she said.

He yanked a handkerchief from his back pocket and mopped his forehead. He turned and surveyed the yard. "It loses its green when you let it go this long." His words had an accusing edge she didn't like.

"Who asked you?" she said. "Did you talk with my daughter? Did you ask if she wanted the lawn mowed? Did she hire you?"

Jeronimo's answer was to start up the mower again. He turned his back and off he went toward the Laytons'. Emily fumed. She didn't know why exactly. She'd been after Alison to have the lawn cut for months. The yard was an absolute embarrassment. But watching it disappear into Jeronimo's huge red machine left Emily feeling as if her veils were being snatched one by one without her permission. There was nothing between her and this unpredictable and volatile man but the ten square feet of tall green grass he'd not yet attacked. Emily waded out into the middle of it. He turned again and came toward her. Sweat beaded on his head and dripped down into the lines of his long face. She watched him grow larger, the mower growling metallically, and held her ground.

When it became clear to him that she was not going to move, he cut the engine. He narrowed his eyes. He smiled with the corners of his mouth. "It's customary to offer lemonade," he said.

"It's customary to ask permission before changing the face of the land," she blurted. She could feel heat in her face.

He looked momentarily flustered, then puzzled. "You wanted the lawn this way?" With the flat of his palm he indicated the ten-foot patch of knee-high grass in which she stood.

"That isn't the point. It's a question of . . . of property rights. Of . . ." She couldn't think what else to say.

"Well, pardon me all to hell," he said, cramming his handkerchief in a wet ball into his back pocket. "I thought I was doing you folks a favor. But, hey!" Up went his big square hands in surrender. "You want your grass, you got your grass." He tilted the mower onto its back wheels and headed toward his camper truck parked at the curb.

"Well, it isn't that—" But he'd sailed out through the gate and pulled the mower with one rough yank into the back of his truck. "Jeronimo?" She went halfway down the path, trying to think what she might say, but he hopped into the cab of the truck and was gone before words could form.

Emily turned toward the house. Her ten feet of grass looked ridiculous, like TC's friend with the green Mohawk sticking straight up in the center of his crew cut, there for no apparent reason but foolish vanity.

She went into the house biting her thumbnail. The man brought out all her worst qualities. Her snobbishness—all that about reading Yeats in French when it wasn't even true. Property rights! Why, Alison would be delighted that someone had cut the lawn. And for free. She wouldn't even ask who or how. The house got cleaned, the children got fed, the laundry got done, the yard got taken care of. It was an everyday kind of magic she had too quickly grown used to.

Samantha was at the kitchen table, head in her arms, sobbing.

"Sam? Whatever is the matter?"

Samantha shook her head. She mumbled something into her arms.

"I can't hear you, Sam. What is it?"

"It's the grass," wailed Sam, lifting a tragic blotchy face swollen with tears. "My grass! He cut it. That stupid man cut all the grass off."

"There, there," Emily said, cradling Sam's head against her stomach. "We can't go crying over cut grass, darling. What's done is done. The horse is out of the barn, so to speak."

"What horse, Nana?"

"Just a saying, darling. Nana's full of sayings today. Hot air, that's all. Why don't you gather up your Barbies and go over to Carrie's? Will that cheer you up?"

Sam took off at a run.

At the sink Emily slid the cellophane off the chicken and washed the pieces in cold water. Through the window she surveyed the new yard. How could she have been so ungracious? The man was doing a simple favor. He was tactless, certainly, but his heart had been in the right place. She'd always laid great store by that.

She would call and apologize. Invite him to something. The symphony. Or a good film. What was the name of that French film showing at the Riviera?

In her mind, she saw once again the imposing figure of Jeronimo Martin Smith coming toward her through the high grass. She saw the way the corners of his mouth turned when he spotted her there on the porch. It was almost as if he'd be giving away too much with a smile. Was he that taciturn, or was he simply shy? As she'd stood in her patch of grass, she was just close enough to smell his sweat. Memory smelled it now. Male sweat. She thought she didn't like it. Well, she supposed it was possible to be stirred by one particular person's . . . odor and not by another's. But she didn't think she ought to be stirred, *unsettled*, by the body odor of someone she didn't like. She thought, at her age, she ought to know better. She dried the chicken parts, smiling.

5

Jeronimo wheeled his BMX 2000 into the garage and dusted it off. Then he oiled it in all the places that might need oiling. He thought that there was probably no need for it, but you couldn't be too careful. Besides, he didn't have that much to do. Not a damned thing that really needed doing. He went inside. The well-lubricated screen door hushed closed behind him.

What had he done so damned wrong? Well, sure, he could have asked her first, but that would have ruined things. He and Emily Parsons would have done this polite little dance, he asking if he might perhaps do her the favor, she hemming and hawing, offering to pay. It wasn't the way he wanted to do it. He wanted to surprise her. He wanted to see the surprise in her eyes and, by that, gauge her interest in him. If there *were* some interest.

Well, he'd found that out all right.

Just as well.

Opening the refrigerator, he rummaged through it, pushing aside Todd's vile health food concoctions, exotic herbs, evil-smelling potions for this or that, he didn't know what all. What was the boy so worried about? He was young.

Sniffing at an open package of sliced ham, Jeronimo carried it and something called Sandwich Spred over to the counter, smeared the Spred on two slices of bread, added a slice of American cheese.

He put the sandwich on a paper towel and took it over to the window. The kitchen was as he liked it, spare and clean as a monk's quarters. After Louise died and a decent time had passed, he'd liberated the room of refrigerator magnets and ruffled curtains, stripped it down and painstakingly refurbished everything. Bare wood floors and cupboard doors now gleamed with an inner light. Each time Todd moved back in, three times in the last four years, Jeronimo had tidied up after him the way he tidied up after himself. It had become a joke, the way Jeronimo would swipe away an unattended coffee cup.

Well, they'd had a few laughs. And Jeronimo had gotten out and about a lot more when Todd was around. Watched him perform at the Ensemble Theatre half a dozen times. He was good. A damned good Mercutio. But then that awful transvestite thing. Todd in green sequins and eyelashes and . . . *breasts.* It had made Jeronimo sick, literally sick in some deep part in which he imagined himself a murderous Abraham, knife drawn to slit the throat of his only son. Surely if there were a God (he went back and forth on this), He would not abide such travesty, such ugly warping of the human spirit.

But Todd was gone, and so that was that. It was harder this time, just why he didn't know, for Jeronimo to acclimate himself to the silence that returned to the four tiny rooms of his house. Something inside him had learned too well to listen for his son, the familiar sounds of his waking, show tunes belted out in the shower, and then, later, the unmistakable sound of his old Volkswagen van, middle of the night, when Jeronimo should have been sleeping. But by then he'd have gotten up five or six times to check the dark windows, and sleep wouldn't come. Every cry of a far-off siren was of course Todd crushed, Todd dead, or worse, dying in some horribly painful way that Jeronimo could do nothing about.

Well, it was no longer appropriate to play father. But to the frustration and embarrassment of both his son and himself, Jeronimo persisted anyway, lectured, harassed, dogged until Todd could stand it no longer. "I'm not a child, Dad," he'd said, as he'd said so many times before. "What the hell are you doing?" But Jeronimo knew that a grown man in full possession of his rational faculties would never make the decisions Todd made, decisions that cost him not only his reputation but risked his very life.

Didn't a father have the right to yank his child back from the edge of a cliff?

Jeronimo took a bite of his sandwich, but his appetite had flattened. He missed Louise, damn it, more than he'd ever thought he would. She was a loud and often crude woman—she'd been a bartender in the days when you rarely saw a woman in a bar, much less behind one—and he'd taken her presence in his life for granted. In the night he would curl around the great round tub of her and sleep like a baby. Now he slept in fits and starts. He'd get up and wander the dark rooms of his house with a cup of warm milk. He was sorry now that he'd tossed every last one of the refrigerator magnets. If he had a wife again, he'd make her take better care of her heart.

It had come to him the night before, as he rolled over to check the digits on his bedside clock, that he was lonely. He wasn't proud of that. A man worth his salt should be self-sufficient. Particularly in his later years when he was likely to be alone. Still, the feeling persisted like an aching tooth.

There was something about Emily Parsons that made him think about things like this instead of what he should be thinking about: getting on the road.

Outside, past the fancy plastic tube feeder to which no bird had ever been attracted, past the lawn precision-edged and trimmed, an unbroken block of green, was his old Ford pickup.

Time to take her on the road. Nothing held him here, that was for sure. On the road he'd drop loneliness behind him like a snake shedding skin. He'd head up to Yellowstone. All his adult life he'd talked about such a trip, threatened as much all his married life, and before long there'd be no more talking to do, except to the daisies. Clear and fixed in his mind like few things had ever been was the only other time he'd been to Yellowstone, that time with his dad when he was ten.

Until that trip the old bastard hadn't been worth much as

a father, or as a husband for that matter. Jeronimo was in his mother's care always, he and Lem. In Jeronimo's mental snapshots his mother stood perpetually at a coal-burning stove stirring something in a heavy iron pot, Lem in a wooden cradle at her feet. His mother's face was misted over, a dark face, smooth as water-worn stone. He did not remember the sound of her voice, he thought now because she so seldom spoke.

Who knew why she'd run off as a teenager with the hard-drinking oil-field worker that had become Jeronimo's father? Perhaps she'd thought a life with him could be no worse than the one she had, and she was right, it wasn't. But it didn't last. When Jared Smith came back through the dirt front yard in August of 1925, they hadn't seen him in more than six years. "Come to get my boy," he said, and Jeronimo's mother, with only a single flashing glance, had let him go.

They'd traveled on horseback. More than the touch of his father's hand, which was brief and shy and seldom, Jeronimo remembered the feel of Jack (short for Jackass, his father said) under his thighs, the miles of country through which they passed, the summer cashing out to fall, cold nights and the smoke of a smoldering campfire.

Unlike his mother, his father talked. When he was drinking, to himself, a running monologue in which he seemed to take two parts — his better self, Jeronimo guessed, in contest with his darker side, the side that won out in the end. But father talked with son as well. Told him stories mostly, stories no boy needed to hear, violent tales in which eyes were torn from live sockets or breasts sliced open in payment for something called "sleeping around." In Jeronimo's mind the stories, incompletely understood, blended and fused into something he recognized now as a great and glorious Bosch pastiche.

It was early winter by the time they reached Yellowstone, and a light snow lay over the vast gray-brown landscape. It was gloomy in a way that could frighten a small boy, though Jeronimo could not put such an unmanly feeling in words. Smoke billowed up from the ground, mud gurgled in tongues, the air smelled of rotten eggs. He worried as Jack clomped steadily along under his aching seat that he had been taken on his father's final ride to hell.

They were gone three months all told. Then his father dropped him back where he'd gotten him and with a wave, his back already turned, disappeared from Jeronimo's life.

As a boy he'd polished the memory of that trip to an unnaturally bright glow, but over time, like old photographs, it faded until only a few distinct images remained. In one, he and his father are making camp. A light snow blows in from across the plains. They have pulled into camp a dried tree branch as fat around as Jeronimo's waist, and his father is stripping it down for a fire. He is efficient, his father. Everything he does has a purpose, every action has a reason. Jeronimo has learned by watching to build a fire in just the right way—there is just the one right way—but his father builds all the fires himself. He is fiercely insistent about this, the whole bulk of him fixed in silent concentration. They will survive the night or they will not, and it will be the father's fire that decides. The boy's eyes follow sparks as they leap into the fading light of the sky. He looks out across the land that he can hold at last without fear. From his father he has learned to think like a frontiersman, to have (or at least pretend to have) the courage of the Apache for whom he was named (with a J for a G because his father knew no better).

Then suddenly, as if by some dreadful magic, a horrible thing rose up before them, materializing intact from the pitch-black night of his worst nightmares. Jeronimo yelped and made to run, but his father's hand came down on his shoulder, pinning him in place. "Shush!" he said. For a time as they watched, the huge bison remained perfectly still in profile against the swirling snow, head lowered, steam rising from its nostrils. Now and then an immense wet black eyeball rolled their way, making Jeronimo flinch. The bison's coat was dull, like the fur of the animals his father shot and wore on his back or tied to his saddle, and it seemed, for the minutes that Jeronimo watched, a sad thing, and he lost all his fear. At last the animal moved off, slowly, searching the ground with its huge snuffling nostrils, moving like planets move, like mountains over time. The animal was starving, his father said, probably sick. The winter would kill it off. Jeronimo was struck to the heart. Couldn't they feed him? He pleaded with his father, pulling angrily on his rough coat, wanting to belt the stupid man who could say such stupid things, watching the animal disappear into the darkness out of which he'd come. How could they let him die? They could gather grass, they could take him to some better place, back to his family. Couldn't they? Couldn't they? But his father said that wasn't the way of nature. Nature picked your time, he said, and when she did you went, if you could, with dignity. Long into the cold night, curled in his blanket roll, Jeronimo kept in his mind's eye the great shaggy shape, dark and dying against the driving snow.

6

Late afternoon, the library hushed as the great cathedrals. Standing just inside the door, Emily thought about those cathedrals—Chartres, Notre Dame. Vaulted ceilings, leaded glass, stone floors that echoed underfoot but that echoed only in her mind. She had seen the wonderful buildings only in picture books. She would never see them now. Something to get weepy about if she chose to. But she couldn't start that. The world was too immense, too full of things she would never see. Instead, she took stock of the main room in her newly adopted small but elegantly appointed public library. Across a Spanish tile floor were several inviting reading tables. An elderly man with a shock of white hair slept upright in one of the chairs, a newspaper spread before him like a picnic cloth. Two teenagers snickered over something they'd found on a computer screen; a slim dark-haired woman moved purposefully behind the reference desk doing what librarians did in the somnolent hours of an October afternoon.

He could be anywhere, of course. If he was here. Upstairs in Fiction, downstairs in Periodicals. Jeronimo Smith didn't spend all his time in the library, certainly. Why did she think she'd find him here? today? this hour? She pinched her lips together in the way she often did when her own behavior disappointed her. Jeronimo Smith wasn't the reason for her visit, she admonished herself. She had two books to return. One was a mystery with the unsatisfying consistency of meringue, the other a five-hundred-page domestic tome she'd have needed another life to finish. Neither offered the hungered-for escape.

She should have just called him up on the telephone. Apologized, as she'd intended. Or not (something about the dead lawn kept getting to her). Told him off, then. "See here, Jeronimo," she'd have said.

See here what? She couldn't very well admit how often she'd thought about him. How often she'd summoned up his image advancing toward her through the high grass, the intensity of those deep-set brown eyes, the wide mouth just shy of a smile. Oh, rather, she could. She was capable of telling him how he made her feel. But she'd risk frightening him away if she did, if she was so forthright. Men were so easily frightened by forward women. Particularly those of his generation, their generation.

And she just might be older than Jeronimo. There was that to consider. He moved with the physicality of a younger man, a man still in touch with the power of his body. She was drawn strongly to it, more strongly than she would have thought possible, to that part of him. To the man that still erupted like an active volcano from his center. And she couldn't very well tell him that.

She marched into the stacks and emerged with a sturdy brown book chosen at random. *Medieval Architecture*, it said in gold letters on the binding. It weighed the same as a bag of potatoes, about five pounds. She lugged it across the room to a reading table in full view of the entrance and settled herself over it in a pose of complete absorption.

But absorption was difficult even to feign. A beam of warm sunlight fell upon the table and upon her head and hands as she turned a musty page full of tiny print and a black-and-white illustration of a bisected wall. Soon she was nodding off and having to snap herself awake. Disgusted with her light-mindedness, Emily pushed the book aside and went guiltily (but happily) after the library's most recent issue of *House and Garden*. She opened it and feasted on the glossy illustrations of decadent gardens and sumptuous expensively decorated sitting rooms meant to look lived in by ordinary people. Two ten, said the great round school clock over the door.

And what would she say if he suddenly appeared?

Well, she could start with an apology. An apology really was in order. What it came down to in the end was that she had been ungrateful.

But perhaps it was too late. Already he'd chalked her up as a mean-spirited shrew. Or worse.

And why should it matter? Why now? When it was too late. Was she still in denial? Hadn't she yet passed into one of the other more useful, sensible stages? She should be reading about that, about dying in the correct order, not about planting gardens she would never get to weed.

Her fingers shook as she turned the glossy magazine pages. But it did matter. It mattered even if one had only a week left, an hour. Being alive mattered. Making plans, anticipating new experiences, savoring, savoring. The heat of the sun in just that place in her neck where her tension housed itself, the sunlit swirls of fine-grained wood beneath her fingertips. It could never cease to matter.

Several times the great wooden entrance door opened. Emily would look up from her magazine with a glance somewhere else, at the clock, at the brightly decorated Children's Section, feigning disinterest, only to see finally that it wasn't him. So burned was he on her inner vision that if he had turned up in the brown perspiration-stained workshirt, hauling his lawn mower she would not have been at all surprised. Each time she heard the door creak, her heart would send up a flare, a signal. Of distress, she was certain. Who would intentionally court this feeling past the age of twelve?

After more of this than she could stand, she gathered up her bag and headed for the door. How silly to think he'd be here on this day, at this time. And she really had expected that he would be. That they were fated, for some reason, to come together. Such was infatuation. Not a quirk of adolescence at all but a mental aberration, an illness. One could be afflicted with it at any age.

Emily pushed through the great doors out onto the sun-flooded flagstone walkway. She would go by Our Daily Bread and pick up a baguette for dinner. That had been her purpose all along, or so she now decided. A loaf of freshly baked bread. Of course! She headed for Santa Barbara Street with purpose in her steps. It was a perfect miracle of an October afternoon. The hem of her blue-and-white dress flipped saucily at her shins. She needed nothing more in life at that moment than a freshly baked baguette.

A horn blared, and she nearly leapt out of her shoes. Jeronimo's faded red truck eased to the curb. "Need a ride, lady?" Like a challenge. He was wearing a blue workshirt, leaning from the steering wheel across the passenger seat.

Her hand had gone straight to her heart. She thought of several things to say, none of them charitable. In fact, her silly heart was thrilled to find him. It cared little about presentation. It wanted to get straight down to business.

He pushed open the door and she climbed in. "I've just been to the library," she said. To look for you, she didn't say.

He checked his side mirror and pulled out into traffic. "Went there myself this morning," he said, looking sheepish. "For research." He glanced over to see if she was buying it. "Yellowstone. Getting ready to take off."

"So!" she cried. "You're really going." Her heart sank. "How wonderful. How long do you expect to be gone?"

He shrugged his broad shoulders. "Who knows? Six months, a year."

Emily pulled her tapestry bag into her middle for comfort. Six months. A year. When she was young that was a lifetime; now she would measure it in heartbeats. "How grand," she said, throwing as much spirit behind her words as she could muster.

"Just driving around," he said, as if she'd asked him to explain his sudden appearance at her heels. "Doing a kind of inventory. Does that make any sense? Ever try to see a place you've lived in half your life like it's the first time?"

"Yes," she said quietly. "When I left Pittsburgh. It suddenly made no sense at all to leave and I nearly canceled my reservation."

"Not me. What I see is a clogged freeway where there was once a two-lane road, a Starbucks instead of the old Copper Coffee Pot, houses the size of battleships perched on the sides of cliffs. Santa Barbara was a sleepy little town when we first moved here. Now it's trying to be Los Angeles. I can't wait to leave it behind."

"But it's enchanting," she protested. "Why, it looks like a village in Spain."

He turned to her. "Been to Spain?"

"Well, no," she admitted. "Sadly, no. Nor France, nor anywhere really."

"Well, I've been to Spain. You're not missing a thing."

She didn't know quite what to say to that—*Barcelona, Granada, The Prado*—so she said nothing.

"That's Todd's elementary school," he said, nodding toward a collection of beige outbuildings gathered within a chain-link fence.

"Todd?"

"My kid. Well, not a kid any longer, of course. His high school's just around the corner." He yanked the wheel left and headed up the block. "There it is," he said. "Damned fine building, one of the few real schools, if you know what I mean. None of those portable shacks they put up now." They passed what was indeed a handsome structure built in Mediterranean style. She wondered why they were visiting his son's schools but didn't ask. Like a tour guide Jeronimo began calling her attention to all the points of interest (and of disinterest—where he took his truck that time to get the brakes fixed and got cheated, where you could get a good cheap pair of sturdy work boots). Then he made a turn into a cemetery. "Louise is here," he said. "Ten years come December."

Emily expected her heart to clutch, given what it might experience as a preview of coming events, but she had always enjoyed cemeteries, and this one was spectacular, with rolling hills, ancient oak trees. Jeronimo stopped at the top of a hill from which they could view the ocean, a deep-blue stripe beneath a band of haze. He cut the engine. As if by prearranged recording, a dozen birds began to sing. "Her family had money," he said. "I couldn't have afforded this." He nodded toward one of the gravesites.

"The ocean view," she said.

"Yeah."

Each turned to sneak a quick look at the other. Jeronimo bit his lip to keep from laughing. "I suppose this is what people really mean when they say they're dying for an ocean view, huh?"

A most indecorous guffaw burst from Emily. She apologized, explaining that Alison's working vocabulary included that exact expression. "But cemetery plots with ocean views!"

"I know, I know," Jeronimo cried. "How crazy can you get?"

"Well, I suppose it's for the living," she said. "The view. For contemplation."

"Look around." Jeronimo turned, surveying the perfectly groomed grounds stretched out before them. "How many contemplators do you see?"

The cemetery appeared to have not a single visitor but themselves. The decorated graves sported fake flowers, the kind that would last far longer than the body beneath the ground. "Would have made a great golf course, if you ask me."

"Which is hers?" Emily asked, scanning the gravesites through her open window. "Louise's?"

"Come on," he said. "I'll show you." His door gave a metallic shriek as he pushed it open. "Been meaning to fix that." He frowned at the offending door. "Too much on my mind lately."

She climbed down out of the truck and followed him up a gravel path to an oak tree whose branches served as an immense umbrella for the gravestones beneath. "There she is," he said. He leaned down, brushing the dry leaves from the headstone bearing the name of his wife and the dates that framed her existence like bookends.

"We should have brought flowers," she said. "Real flowers."

"I haven't been here since the day she was buried," he said, working his jaw. "Never made much sense to me. Louise and I . . ." He tilted his head back, scanned the cloudless blue sky for words. "We toughed it out, I guess you could say. She told me straight when we got married that she'd never have done it, except for Todd. He was, as they said then, a little premature. Six months premature. We did what was expected. She was a good woman."

Emily read the inscriptions on the graves flanking Louise's. "Won't you be buried by her side?"

"Not me. Can't afford the real estate. How about you? Got a plot somewhere?"

"No," she said. "I've never much cared about where I end up."

He nodded. "Neither do I. What does it matter who's next to you or where your bones are?"

"Or your ashes."

"Together for all eternity and all that hogwash."

"Hogwash." She'd said it in the way he did, all wind and bluster, but he didn't catch on.

"I'm glad you agree," he said.

"But I don't," she said. "Not entirely. There's nothing wrong with the impulse that makes us long to mingle our ashes after death. It may be futile—after all, who knows what happens after this? But the desire, that's the thing. The deep need to never let go. Think of *Wuthering Heights*!"

"Talk about your over-imaginative pieces of tripe."

"*Wuthering Heights*? Why, it's a classic. One of the great love stories of all time."

"Catherine! Catherine!" cried Jeronimo, flinging his arms at the placid blue sky.

"Why, there's not a romantic bone in your body, Jeronimo Smith," laughed Emily.

He composed himself and stood looking at her for several seconds, his long arms hanging at his sides. "I could surprise you," he said, more quietly than she'd ever heard him speak.

She turned away, a smile tugging at her lips. In another second she'd be blushing like a girl.

They walked down the path side by side. "I don't know why we ended up here," he said when they were back in the truck. He stared out through the windshield with the most puzzled expression.

"Saying good-bye?" Emily suggested.

He turned to her and his face cleared. He seemed to come awake. "I guess that's it. But I didn't have to bring you." He started the engine. "Sorry about that." Dismissively, as if to someone outside the truck.

"Are you?"

Surprised, he turned. His eyes were caught in hers and couldn't seem to break away. "Why, no," he admitted. "No, I guess I'm not."

They drove back across town in a companionable silence. Something had been resolved, Emily didn't know what it was, only that it was evident in Jeronimo's face and in the set of his shoulders. It came to her then that he must have another woman in his life, several others. He was everything every silly woman wanted, strength mixed with baffling inscrutability. She didn't want to be among the silly women, but it was too late.

They came to the sagging gate of Alison's house too soon. Jeronimo pulled up to the curb and cut the engine. "I could finish off the lawn," he said with an engaging grin. "Wouldn't take a minute."

She smiled up at him. "I think we'll leave it as it is."

"Emily," he said, his face working itself into an agonized frown. "Emily, I—" He sighed, turned away, looked back, his thumb drumming the steering wheel. "Look," he said. "Emily."

"Yes?"

"I think you oughta come with me." As if he were looking straight into the sun and not her expectant face, he squinted. "I think you should."

"Come with you?"

"To Montana," he said. "To Yellowstone."

"Oh!" She laughed, a short huff of surprise. "Well. Yellowstone." Buying time. Already an errant part of herself, the part she'd kept under wraps for decades, was flapping its atrophied wings. "Well, of course I can't. But, *well*. What an offer. I can't imagine—"

"No," he said quietly, looking out through the windshield at a scattering of noisy, brightly dressed children returning from school. "No, of course you couldn't."

When he turned her way again she could see the spark had gone out of him.

"It's the children, you see," she hastened to explain. "Sam and TC. They've come to count on me. And Alison, of course . . ."

"Well, sure. It was just an idea."

He seemed to fling the whole thing off with a jerk of his chin, as if to say it had all been whim after all. Nothing serious. A spontaneous thing. He hadn't really meant it. After all, they hardly knew each other.

But Emily couldn't somehow open the door and get out of the truck. She sat looking down at her arms clasped around her purse, as if she were physically holding the whole of her self back. From what? Excitement? Life?

"I mean, how could I just . . . just up and go? Like that? At my age? It's irresponsible."

"Reckless."

"Flighty. Inconsiderate."

She laughed because he was laughing. With her, at her.

"Footloose."

". . . and fancy free," she finished, her voice sad with longing.

"Well, can't say I didn't try," he said. "I'll send you a postcard."

"Do that," she said brightly. "I'll picture you sleeping out under the stars."

She didn't say how often and in how many other ways she would see him in her imagination.

"Well." He cleared his throat.

"Yes." She fumbled for the door handle.

He leaned across her lap to push the handle for her. His shoulder skimmed her chin, crossed her breast, and her arms, suddenly weak, dropped away from her purse. The door fell open. He pulled back.

"Take care of yourself, Emily Parsons," he said. "Don't let those kids wear you out."

She stood outside the truck, one hand on the door ready to push it closed. Behind her—she could feel it—the house loomed.

"Good-bye, Jeronimo," she said, her throat thick. "Do send that card."

She pushed the door, but it wouldn't close. He reached across and yanked it hard, a final sound. He gave her a two-finger salute, then cranked the engine and drove off down the tree-shaded street.

Emily stood in the warm exhaust, watching until the red truck with its white metal camper box was indistinguishable from its surroundings. She felt drained, empty, as if her life were leaking out through her rubber soles straight into the ground.

7

Jeronimo filled the two small cupboards with food from the kitchen: oatmeal, dried prunes, canned beans, things that would keep. Probably should have taken up hunting at one point or another in his life, but it was too late now. He would just eat a lot of fish. The double cabover bunk was made up in military fashion, with sheets tight enough to bounce a coin on. The red Naugahyde on the narrow single bed and the seats of the banquette was cracked and worn but would last as long as he did. Not much else to do but take off.

Why had he thought she'd come with him? A woman like that, as self-contained as his camper. Why would a woman like that want to put up with a temperamental codger like him?

Reasonable adults didn't run off together half-cocked. He'd

have been sorry if she'd said yes. He'd have been sick with anxiety. He no longer knew how to act around women. And a woman like her.

Still rationalizing in his mind what could very well have turned into a disaster, he locked the camper door and went inside. On the TV, George Bush was going to war with Saddam Hussein. Jeronimo eased himself into his old green corduroy recliner to watch his president. Age had its advantages, and this was one of them. Neither he nor George would ever fight another war. It was far easier to be patriotic if you weren't the point man. Probably should have a TV in the camper to follow the news as this thing escalated. Well, he could read the newspaper. But did he want to? He didn't think so. He would let George fight this one himself.

He got up and went to the liquor cabinet. The thought of young men being sent into war was enough to ruin a good Jack Daniel's. He poured himself two fingers over ice and eased down in the recliner again.

The thing was that the woman, Emily Parsons, had revived something inside him that had long lain fallow. He didn't have a name for it. Didn't want to name it. A sensation, swirling around like a loose turnip in the stewpot of his feelings. It wasn't comfortable, this feeling. He'd rather not have it, given the choice, but here he was, stuck with it. It was what happened when one let one's guard down for the briefest time.

All well and good to take up with some woman his age for rounds of golf and bouts of bridge, maybe an occasional roll in the hay if it came to that. But he wanted something more. And for some reason he thought Emily Parsons might want it too. Something more. He wanted someone beside him as the nights grew long, someone to be there when he was sick, or worse. Someone there at the end.

That was what it came down to, he supposed, nothing erotic or kinky. Just somebody there at the end. Was that too much to ask?

Emily laid her book down on the bedside table. She'd read an entire page of the best-seller without registering a single word. Downstairs she could hear Alison on the telephone, hammering out a deal she'd made, or was trying to make. Ten past nine. The children were watching a video—something violent, by the sound of it, with thunderous explosions, cars and people flying through the air on fire. Dreadful. Sam and TC had bickered their way through dinner, Emily refereeing while Alison dialed the telephone. Which was fast becoming ritual. She had been drawn into the joylessness of her daughter's household and could do little to change it.

Outside her window the sky was ink black and empty. Emily closed her eyes and saw a red truck with a shabby white camper box driving off into mountains. But the mountains were as manufactured as those on the television. She had never seen Montana. In her geographic ignorance, she'd often confused Yosemite with Yellowstone and didn't know much about either one. And now she never would.

She could have gone with him. In a blink of an eye, she'd have been ready. In her closet her suitcase was already packed for the hospital, whenever her time came. She could have grabbed it up packed as it was with its brand-new toothbrush (why?), its tube of toothpaste (the sample size, no need for more), and run off with Jeronimo. If only she had courage. But all she'd done was confirm that the last trip of her life would be to a sick ward. That's what she was ready for, she with her cowardice, her excuses. Death, not adventure. She reached over and switched off the light. Turning on her side, she watched the blue neon numbers on her bedside clock tick away with astonishing determination the minutes of her life.

Jeronimo awoke to some fool who was down on all fours sucking whipped cream out of a dog's mouth. "We'll break for a commercial," David Letterman said, "then it's back for more stupid pet tricks." Jeronimo punched the off button. The room was dark. The whiskey had left his mouth stale. He was stiff from sleeping in an upright position. He'd drooled down the front of his shirt.

Should have been on the road by now, and here he was napping, as if he weren't going anywhere at all. All afternoon he'd been hyped up, readying the camper like a space capsule for departure. That had been the fun part. Now there was nothing left to do but go. Well, get up, he told himself. Get on with it. But his body didn't seem to want to move. "One of these days . . ." he'd threatened whenever life (son or wife) got too demanding. Now there was no one to threaten. When he left no one would be waving tearfully at the door. One of these days was here.

He padded into the bathroom in his socks, switched on the light, shuddered at the sight of his bloodshot eyes, flicked off the light. There was moon enough to brush his teeth by. In his bedroom, he pulled his hiking boots from the back of the closet.

Later he told himself that it was the ladder that did it, that spoke to him. But that was just another excuse. The fact was, he couldn't stop thinking about her. Jeronimo had slid open the garage door, and there was the ladder laid along a side wall. It was a new aluminum ladder purchased in expectation of painting the house come spring. He hoisted it onto the top of the camper and secured it with bungee cords.

"There," he said, though he didn't exactly know why. "That'll do it."

He crossed town, ignoring most of the stop signs. Not a soul in the streets. He passed only one car, navigated by a body with two heads. At second glance, just a couple of kids. He'd had a car like that once, the kind you could snuggle your sweetie in, but he was married by then and past snuggling.

He cut the engine where Anapamu crossed Laguna and coasted half a block to a stop. The moon was three-quarters full, and the cottage stood out in bold relief against its clipped lawn nearly as if it were daylight. He could make out the number 467 on the door frame where the paint was curling off. He'd have had to paint the whole damned house if he'd stayed around much longer.

The truck door shrieked open. Jeronimo waited, alert, and when no lights came on, stepped down onto the street. He'd have preferred a dark night, cloud cover, but the moon shone down like a spotlight in a prison compound. He'd have to make a run across the treeless side yard, the lawn he himself had sheared.

What if there was a dog? He hadn't considered that. She hadn't mentioned a dog, but then why would she? Just then, with the ladder half slid from the roof of the camper, the million things Jeronimo didn't know about Emily Parsons descended like thick soup to stop his forward motion. But it was too late. He'd made his decision. Now he couldn't imagine doing this any other way, going back to the other life already behind him, his recliner, Todd's empty room. After a quick look around the dark neighborhood, he shouldered the ladder and made a dash for it.

Emily bolted straight up in bed. If it hadn't been for the moonlight gleaming off a now familiar bald head, she'd have screamed. Instead, she pulled the comforter to her chin, what women facing imminent attack generally did. Whatever good that would do. And yet she knew, eccentric as Jeronimo Smith surely was, that she was safe. She chuckled at the pure craziness of an elderly man, a senior citizen, standing at the window of her second-story bedroom.

His palms went up and down pantomiming the opening of a window. Was he in some kind of trouble? More likely he'd just gone the rest of the way round the bend. She could understand that.

She swung her feet over the side of the bed and put her slippers on. She arranged her nightgown. Light and evanescent, her stomach full of bubbles, she went to the window. There was no mistaking the gleaming head and shaggy eyebrows, the impatient look in the eyes. "Hold your water," she said, more to herself than to him, since he could not hear her. "Hold your water." She unlatched the window and pushed it up. He came through, one long leg at a time, like a spider. "Careful," she whispered. "Careful, you'll hit your . . ." Bang went his forehead. He grabbed it and bit his lip to restrain the dozen epithets he generally attributed to inanimate objects that didn't behave.

"What on earth are you doing?" she demanded when he was standing full height on her braided rug rubbing his forehead. Her nightgown was thick flannel, a shapeless sack from chin to ankle, a deterrent to attack if ever there was one. Still, the impropriety of the occasion gave pause now that he was actually in her bedroom. "What are you doing this time, Jeronimo? Washing windows?"

He towered over her in his dark clothes looking completely out of place and more than a little disoriented. Hers was a perfectly reasonable question, one he should have expected. Still, he took his time answering it, saying the words out loud, with all the emphasis they needed to convince her. "You've got to come with me, Emily." And then, because he thought she might have forgotten, he added: "To Montana."

She stared up at a face that had become for some reason or other uncannily familiar. It was an open face, the perpetually surprised face of someone who'd blundered again and again into parties to which he'd never been invited, and he'd made, with his bluster and orneriness, an almost indelible impression on her. There was more to him than he met the world with.

"Sit," she said, and backed him into her reading chair. The room seemed too small to hold all of him, and he was clumsy in it. He sat

in the chair with his feet splayed out. "Collect yourself. Now . . ."
She turned on her bedside lamp and the walls bloomed cabbage
roses. "Tell me, calmly, what this is all about. Why you have to go.
Why I should go with you."

He leaned forward, arms dangling between his legs, hands
clutched together. Salt-and-pepper eyebrows had bunched themselves together over the long hooked nose; the deep brown eyes
were serious and purposeful. "We're muttering along, Emily. Both
of us. Let's face it."

"Muttering?"

He ignored her amused smile. "When was the last time you
did something exciting, or crazy, or just . . . *something* because you
wanted to do it? No thought about anybody else. What they'd think
about it. The way you do when you're young."

"When you're a child, yes. An adolescent, a rebellious teenager—"

"Bull crap, Emily!" He shot up out of the chair and paced the few
yards to the opposite side of the room and back. He ran his hand
over his head, glancing sheepishly in her direction. "Well, damn it,
that's what it is. I've done my part. I've been a good citizen, paid a
half century of taxes. I've been a decent husband, a father. I even
got myself shot in the butt for my country. Now it's my turn to enjoy what's left of my life. And you," he said, turning to her now
with an intensity that left her shaking because it seemed in that
moment that he knew what he could not possibly know. "You're
living here like a . . . a servant. Like you have another fifty years to

change things. Life is short, Emily. It's a damned cliché, isn't it? But it's the truth. Let's just live the rest of it for ourselves."

Tears sprang suddenly to Emily's eyes and she looked away. Down the hall her grandchildren slept, TC grinding his teeth, Sam splayed in all directions.

She turned shakily to Jeronimo, who stood with his fingers on the window ledge as if ready to bound into the air like Superman, with or without her. At the clinic she hadn't asked, intentionally, how long before the end. Now she wished that she had. It would be easier to parcel out what was left of her life. Part to this wild man, to whom one portion of her being seemed already joined. Part to family, to Alison who still needed her, and to the children.

It occurred to Emily, as it had from time to time, but never for long, that the equation was off somehow. That there always should have been a piece for herself. Yet she struggled against owning it, owning up to it. Jeronimo's eyes had settled into hers and, for a moment, softened. Did he know this struggle? She didn't think so. But perhaps he could understand it. She could fly with him if she could just let go of all the old rules, the phantom voices and faces that made her who she was.

"I'll go with you," she said. "I will!"

"You will? Are you sure?" He took a step back, like the highest bidder at an auction with a sudden case of buyer's remorse.

"Turn around," she said.

"Huh?"

"Turn your back so I can dress."

He listened to the sounds she made as she scurried around be-hind him. Second thoughts bloomed like the posies on her wall. What had he done? What had seemed a bright idea just a short time ago seemed ridiculous now. And what was she doing going along with a ridiculous idea? Perhaps she wasn't as smart as he'd thought. What kind of a woman would drop everything and run off with a man she hardly knew? He'd turn around and call it off, that's what he'd do. Say it was all a little joke. To get to know her better. Or something. But it was too late and he knew it. Panic rose in his throat and threatened to cut off his wind.

"Ready," she said, and he turned to see her dressed in blue jeans and a pale yellow sweater, suitcase in hand. Her wiry curls were covered with a bright blue scarf. It hadn't taken her five minutes. Did she do this kind of thing all the time? "We'll have to be very quiet going down the stairs," she warned, "so we don't wake the children."

"This way," he said, indicating the open window. There was more than one way to skin a cat. She'd never do it. She'd never go out the window and down that ladder.

"Not on your life. I'd break my neck." But she said it with a little smile, as if she was more amused than alarmed that a woman her age might climb out the window like a teenager. "Well, why not?" she said, peering out over the windowsill. "We might as well start off on even ground. Even if I have to fall on it."

"I'll go first," he said, a little stunned by her bravery, then buoyed by it. "I'll steady the ladder for you."

"Wait," she cried. "What was I thinking of?" She snatched a pen from the drawer of her desk. "Dear Lord," she muttered, "what do I tell the children?" But the right words popped instantly into her mind like a going-away present. She wrote several lines on a sheet of scented writing paper, slipped the note into an envelope, and laid it on her pillow.

8

Emily watched Santa Barbara fall past the window of the truck. The shops at night looked a little forlorn, smaller and less sophisticated than they did during the day. What appeared at first to be a bundle of rags turned out to be a homeless person asleep in the doorway of Kernohan's toy shop. Alison said the homeless were bringing down property values and causing shoppers to take their business elsewhere. But where were they to go, Emily wondered. Alison didn't have an answer to that.

A sickening wave of panic washed through Emily. What in the world had she done? What turmoil was she leaving in her wake? Alison would have to miss work while she searched for a suitable sitter (none ever lasted), the children's behavior (what small part she had influenced) would relapse into unruliness, the hospital would have to find another part-time volunteer for the reception desk, her friends would have to be told something. By someone. Eventually. But in the end, all Emily considered was herself. The surprise of that lingered as she stole a glance at Jeronimo. What she had considered most in those last moments at 467 Laguna was what lot she had remaining to her, what little she had left. She expected to feel the anguish that generally accompanied decisions made solely in the interest of oneself, but what she felt instead was exhilaration.

"I thought we were going to Montana," she said as Jeronimo turned south on the freeway.

"We are."

"But Montana is north," she said. So Jeronimo had the chance to explain why, because of the Sierra, you went south to get north, which was a conversation of sorts and a metaphor to his way of thinking for the way Californians lived, and things got easier between them. He spoke formally, as if they had just met. She forced herself to swallow her misgivings, to think about the adventure ahead.

Las Vegas would be their first stop, he said. That was about as long as he could hold out. Had she ever been there? She said she hadn't. She didn't think she'd like Las Vegas, but she didn't tell him that. Over the steady growl of the engine she told Jeronimo some things about the children because they were still so clearly on her mind. "TC's a soccer star," she said, "and Samantha's into everything, gymnastics, ballet. They do well in school, well enough. I just wish they were more interested in books, in ideas. They seem to have no natural curiosity. Things just wash over them somehow. Do you know what I mean?"

"That's the way it is now," he said. A motor home the size of a Greyhound bus passed, and passed, on the left. There were fancy bicycles strapped onto it and a small blue sedan in tow. WE'RE SPENDING OUR CHILDREN'S INHERITANCE said a bumper sticker pasted to the back window. "And it's not just the kids either. Nobody's got imagination. Nobody reads. Everybody's looking for some Rambo movie to stumble into."

"And missing the movie they're already in. Exactly."

They turned to each other and smiled wholeheartedly for the first time, each pleased with the other's ability to perfectly capture what was wrong with present-day America.

"What shall we call our movie?" she mused.

"Huh?"

"How about *Jeronimo's Big Sky?*"

Jeronimo shot her a half-amused sideways glance. He cleared his throat but didn't answer her. Had she embarrassed him? Well, she didn't know the man, not yet. Her heart fell away from its playful mood. She drew her sweater more tightly around her shoulders.

"Sam would love this," she said, half to herself. "She runs away from home just for adventure."

"Is that safe?"

"Oh, yes. She just runs off and hides somewhere nearby. I pack her a lunch to take along."

"Who'll watch the kids now?" Jeronimo asked.

"One of the neighborhood teenagers, I expect. That's how it was before I came. The children have always had nannies or gone to child care—"

"Shouldn't have them in the first place," Jeronimo spouted. Emily was beginning to enjoy the timbre of Jeronimo's voice and thought she might find a way to tell him. That way he might not be so prone to raising it.

"Children? You don't mean that."

"I just don't happen to think everybody's fit to be a parent just because they have the equipment to make babies. Nobody knows about how much work it is to raise kids. And self-sacrifice. And how, after you think you've got the job done, the whole thing blows right up in your face!"

"What whole thing?" She wished he wouldn't pound the steering wheel for punctuation.

"And the demands. Why, it never stops. My kid was living with me until just two weeks ago. Mooching. Forty-seven years old and he shows up on his old man's doorstep, everything he owns in a laundry basket."

Emily watched Jeronimo in profile as he went on with his petty complaints about his grown son. Jeronimo Smith was an altogether imposing figure with his prominent nose and slick bald head. He seemed too large for the cab of the small truck, and yet he appeared to be wedded to it out of, she supposed, some long history. When he wasn't pounding the steering wheel, he held it loosely at its base, with a confidence that told her she was safe. What choice had she, anyway? She no longer drove a car herself. Probably should have told him that ahead of time.

"Just the one son?" she asked.

"Todd. Yes. Just the one." And then he began going on about Louise. He described her in a rather odd way, much like a character in a novel: hair and eye color (blond, hazel), the way she wore her hair in "that funny neck roll." He said he never liked it that way but that he'd never told her either. "No wonder she never changed it," he blurted, turning to Emily as if realizing suddenly that she was still there.

Two motorcycles zipped past, their riders hunched like turtles. "Well, it's all gone to hell," Jeronimo pronounced finally. Emily tried to think what to say next, how to keep the conversation going.

"Your son . . . Todd. What does he do?"

Jeronimo said nothing for several seconds. Then he said his son was involved in theater. In San Francisco. But he sounded angry about it. Perhaps he had plans for his son, Emily guessed. Some business venture that didn't work out the way he'd expected. She gave Jeronimo space to continue, but he seemed not to want to say anything more.

The ocean running along the side of the freeway was pooled like black ink and rippled with moonlight. Emily stared out into it and thought about children, about the dreams she'd had for her own. Losing Evan had been, for her and for Frank, the end of dreaming, of believing one could bend destiny to desire. "He'd have been forty-four this June," she said. "Imagine . . ."

"What?" Jeronimo had been mired in thought as well.

"Hmmm? Oh! I didn't realize I'd spoken. Just thinking."

Silence became easier than trying to manufacture conversation. She'd begun to drift off when he startled her with the news that after stopping a day in Las Vegas they'd be visiting his brother. His brother, Lemuel, his name was, lived at a place called Sunnyrest with his wife, Shirley. Emily was disappointed. Rest homes weren't included on her itinerary of adventures. But when he said he hadn't seen his brother in twenty years, she decided to say nothing.

After a while she asked if they might stop soon.

"Stop?"

"At a restroom." Had he planned on barreling all the way to Las Vegas without stopping?

In the women's bathroom Emily shook two capsules from one of the brown plastic bottles in her purse and washed them down with a palm full of water. She splashed water on her face, patting it dry with a rough paper towel.

The thing was, she felt fine, considering. Didn't look like much, but what did she expect? She'd already outlived most land mammals. It was a bit disquieting to accept that the face in the yellowed light of a gas station mirror was her own. All this should be a dream, a troubled dream in which she'd been kidnapped, torn bodily, screaming, from the arms of her family. Instead, inside where she'd husbanded all her caution over the years was this single live ember.

Emily pinched some color into her cheeks and left the restroom.

"You can get a coffee or something inside if you want," Jeronimo said shortly when she returned. Garish lights and neon killed what had begun to sprout in the darkened cab. He sounded gruff now, as if he might have changed his mind about her in the five minutes of her absence.

"Nothing, thanks."

They pulled onto the highway and headed off again into the darkness. After a while Emily began to nod off. Once, she awoke with the humiliating certainty that she'd been snoring. Then she fell deeply into sleep.

She awoke from an anxious dream in which she'd been a much younger self, a young matron. She was giving a dinner party, hundreds of people seated at picnic tables, only the tables were inside the house in a dozen separate rooms and she had to serve everybody herself. They'd been rude and unappreciative, claiming to be devout vegetarians when all she'd made was beef Bourguignonne. Awake, she was glad to be rid of them, though she didn't know quite where she was. In a car. In a supermarket parking lot. Cars on all sides in neat, endless rows. Then memory returned.

She climbed down from the pickup, surprisingly alert for having slept with her head against a rattling window. She stretched her arms. Far above her, a diamond-studded high-heeled shoe the size of a small plane revolved slowly against a pink-tinged night sky. The building below was splashed with light, colored lights that beamed or shot in all directions. Crossing the parking lot, remembering all the carnivals of her youth, Emily wondered why she had decided in advance not to like Las Vegas.

At the entrance to the Silver Slipper she stepped through a bank of glass doors into what her hardshell Baptist parents would have called the pits of hell. It was garish as an old-time saloon, with red carpets and gold flocked wallpaper. Overhead a dozen chandeliers glittered, and a ricky-tick piano played Scott Joplin's "Maple Leaf Rag," though you could barely make out the tune for the racket of the slot machines. Emily descended into it, hugging her purse, scanning the room for Jeronimo's bald head. A cocktail waitress zipped past on very long legs. The seams in her black stockings ran like exposed veins into the full cups of half-bare buttocks. Emily stared after her, but there were dozens of other things just as startling to snare her attention, and she wandered through aisles of slot machines and gaming tables in a trance. Buzzers buzzed, bells rang, coins clattered, everything sparkled and flashed and made you see double. Suspended from the ceiling was an actual car, a shiny red convertible bound up with a wide white ribbon. You could win it for a quarter. Emily decided there must be some trick to it.

A loud buzzer went off in her right ear. A woman about her age began scooping silver dollars from the bin of her machine and stacking them into plastic trays. There appeared to be hundreds of dollars in those trays by the time she finished, but the woman never cracked a smile. She might as well have been a bank teller counting someone else's money.

Impulsively, Emily fished a quarter from her change purse, put it into the slot of an open machine and pulled the handle. Reels spun and clunked into place, two cherries and a plum. A subdued buzzer sounded and five quarters dropped into the bin.

"Drink?" This waitress had flaming orange hair and tarantula eyelashes. She looked to be all of sixteen, a child in dress-up clothes. The man next to Emily ordered scotch. He seemed to be having a terrible time. His forehead was scrunched. He sweated profusely, his Hawaiian print shirt stuck to his back. Emily put one quarter into her wallet and three into the machine. Now that she was playing with company money, she was feeling reckless, but when her machine began shrieking like a runaway ambulance, she leapt back in alarm.

"Jackpot!" the man said, jumping up from his stool. "You hit the fucking jackpot!" He looked to be on the verge of tears. But surely he was wrong. Not a coin had clattered out of the slot beneath the machine.

A small crowd began to gather. "Congratulations, honey," said a woman dressed in black slacks and vest. Her name tag said Vilma. North Carolina. A similarly clad man had fit a key into the machine and was tinkering with its insides.

"What did I do?" asked Emily.

"You won two hundred and fifty dollars," the woman said and handed over a stack of plastic trays. Coins began thundering into the bin.

"Can't I just have bills?" she said. "I'll never be able to carry all this."

Vilma frowned, then seemed to realize that Emily was a legitimate greenhorn. She offered to help carry the coins to the cashier's cage. "They'll try to give it to you in chips," she said. "But that's just so you'll drop it on the table. House doesn't like to see anybody walk out with cash."

"Oh, dear," Emily said.

"Screw 'em," Vilma said. "It's your dough. You earned it."

Emily didn't think she had. A quarter and ten minutes of her time wasn't exactly honest work.

"Place'll screw ya blind, let me tell ya. They haven't given a raise around here since the Civil War. And my kid's talking college. Can you beat that? College. And me with an eighth-grade education."

"You must be proud," Emily said. "My daughter never made much of college. She doesn't read books, you see. What's your daughter's name?"

"Liddie. Short for Lydia. She was a twin. The other one didn't make it." Vilma had stopped short of the cashier's cage, the plastic trays aloft, her eyes overcast with memory.

"I lost one, too," Emily said. "A son. It's hard, isn't it?"

Vilma came out of her fog, momentarily off balance. She looked sharply into Emily's eyes, then the look in her own eyes softened in response to something she saw there.

"Lady wants cash," she said to the cashier, who spread five brand-new fifty-dollar bills in a fan across the counter. "You put that away for something nice," Vilma said, patting Emily's hand. "Something for yourself. Good things don't happen every day, you know."

"Not every day," said Emily. "But most days have a little something, don't they?"

Vilma's smile was weary but genuine. "You're a real corker, you know that?"

"Am I? What a lovely thing to say."

Emily found Jeronimo at a poker table scowling down at five

cards spread in the cave his big hands made. There were a half dozen other men and a woman at the table, all gloomy as pallbearers. At Jeronimo's elbow were three red and two yellow chips. It didn't look like much. Emily peered over his shoulder.

"Save the eights," she whispered. Jeronimo jumped. When he turned, she saw she'd really startled him. He appeared at first not even to recognize her. "Eights are lucky," she said.

"Not for Doc Holiday," he said. "I thought you'd still be asleep."

"Play 'em or fold 'em," the dealer said.

Jeronimo laid his cards facedown, gathered his chips, and stood. "Not my night," he said.

"Don't be so sure," she said.

He was every bit as surprised as she'd hoped he would be by her windfall. "I think we should stay here. What do you think? We'll have room service. Champagne!"

His eyes lit up, then just as quickly faded. "Well," he said. "Well, I don't know."

"Why not?" she said. "What's stopping us? Is it the money? Do you want to save it for something else?"

"It's not the money," he said.

"Then what?"

But he couldn't seem to come up with anything.

"Oh, come on," she said. "You're the one who said we had to live it up."

"Sorry, don't have a thing," said the front desk clerk. "Except the honeymoon suites. Don't suppose you're on honeymoon or nothin'." He grinned at his own little joke through a set of ill-fitting teeth.

Emily, still high, glanced at Jeronimo and said, "We'll take it." Only after they'd gathered the luggage and gone halfway down the hallway toward the elevator did it occur to her that, of *course*, a honeymoon suite would have only one bed. Probably not even a very big bed. Perhaps she had enough money for a second room.

Two rumpled old folks looking tired and disoriented met them head-on as the elevator opened on the fourth floor. It took a few seconds for Emily to recognize herself in the wall-to-ceiling mirrors. It was the same all the way down the hall. Did people really want to see themselves coming and going? Or was that just the fancy of some Hollywood decorator? Jeronimo stalked ahead as if the mirrors, and Emily, weren't there.

At 402 he fit a punched card into the lock and opened the door. Emily's laugh erupted like a bark. The room had been done up like a brothel, with mirrored walls and silver wallpaper. Even the swag curtains drooped like women in fixed poses of suggestive abandon. "Oh, Lordy, look at this!" laughed Emily, crossing the room. At her feet was a steaming heart-shaped pink Jacuzzi. But Jeronimo couldn't move. His mouth had fallen open. His neck felt flushed. "Oh, where's your sense of humor, Mo?" she said.

He came out of his trance and blinked several times. "Mo?"

"Is that all right? 'Jeronimo' is such a mouthful."

She peered down at the telephone, then took her reading glasses out of her purse and placed them on the end of her nose. She punched the button for room service. "We'll have a bottle of champagne," she said into the receiver. "Oh, the French, of course. And some . . . some caviar!"

Jeronimo's mortification gave way to surprise. No one but his father had ever called him Mo. Not a single soul. Something loosened inside. He felt warm, as if he were going to be sick. Then he realized that was how you felt just before you began to cry. It had been so long he'd forgotten. He blinked, feeling like a moron, yet feeling at the same time a helpless kind of gratitude. He needed her so much that it paralyzed him. He couldn't let her know, didn't know where to begin.

"I don't like caviar," he said, even more gruffly than he'd intended.

"Neither do I," she said evenly. "It's just something you have to do."

Jeronimo pulled open the double closet doors and stared in. "Who needs all this space?" he grumbled.

The champagne arrived in a silver bucket on a silver tray. Yellow rosebud in a silver vase. Emily pronounced it "perfect." Jeronimo thought it stuffy and pretentious. Champagne. *French* champagne. He didn't know how much to write down for a tip. The whole two-fifty was probably shot already. He saw himself across the room in the mirror, an Ichabod Crane in khaki work pants and worn blue windbreaker, towering over the waiter. He hadn't fully realized before this how prominent was the gleaming prominence of his head. Until now it hadn't mattered. But she was so . . . *refined.* Right at home with silver trays and caviar. He watched her pour champagne into two crystal glasses, her back straight as the Queen Mother's. She was trim and quick and saw the bright side of things. What could she possibly see in him? He felt a stirring in parts he'd considered strictly utilitarian for the past half dozen years. It surprised and embarrassed him, but the feeling passed like the half-forgotten memory of a favorite birthday. He scribbled his name on the check. The waiter bowed several times going out the door, but Jeronimo didn't find that at all amusing. A two-buck tip should be enough for anyone. All he did was roll a cart down the hall.

"What shall we drink to?" Emily asked. Jeronimo stared at the hand offering the glass. He'd noticed before that she wore no fingernail polish or jewelry, a sign of good taste in his book. Now the hand looked naked, vulnerable.

"Well," he hesitated, cleared his throat, and did the best he could. "To smooth roads and good weather."

"Oh, how pedestrian," she cried. "To Emily Parsons and Jeronimo Smith. To second and third childhoods. To adventure!"

"While it lasts," he said, just to keep things in perspective. There was no way to know how long she would put up with him.

"While it lasts," she agreed with a slight catch in her voice.

When they'd finished their glasses of champagne and nibbled at the caviar (she pronounced it "not so bad," he said it "stunk"), she leaned back against the pillows of the huge bed and yawned.

"I'll just go down to the camper," Jeronimo offered quickly, having rehearsed the line several times already in his head. "You can have the bed."

"Don't be silly," she said. "We're not children, after all. We're two grown people, and there's plenty of room in this monster of a bed for both of us."

She took her suitcase into the bathroom and left him staring like a bridegroom at the satin coverlet and pillow slips, one already indented with the shape of Emily's small head.

He walked several times from the bed to the window and looked down at the aqua eye of the swimming pool. Once, it seemed to wink up at him. She seemed a bit frisky for a woman her age. Perhaps she was interested, or could get interested. But did he want her to? Did he want to? Panic rose again in his throat. The last time he tried . . . well, he tried. That was about it. Had been terrified ever since of running into the woman—Rose, her name was, a perfectly nice woman, friend of a friend—in the supermarket. Afraid she'd offer up, in memory of their time together, a wilted carrot to counter the bunch of insouciant bananas in his shopping cart. He'd thought all this was behind him. It wasn't worth it. Never thought he'd say it and never would aloud, but the whole sex thing wasn't worth the anxiety. Besides, at his age and hers! You had to guard your heart.

Emily locked the bathroom door behind her. The lights were too bright. Garish. They cast over her face a sickly green pall that she turned away from, shaken. She'd managed for quite long stretches to forget that she was dying. She'd reminded herself that everyone was dying. That they simply didn't know when. But then she'd catch a glimpse of her frightened face, and her rationalizations would fall away like so much shucked corn.

She stepped quickly out of her clothes, folding them on the toilet seat, and without glancing back into the mirror stepped into the hot shower. What must he be thinking? She'd run off with him like some flighty teenager, with hardly a backward glance, and here she was ready to leap into bed. She lathered the washrag and scrubbed it over her body, automatically, just as she'd done for eight decades, left armpit before the right, back of the neck, then the right ear.

For so many, many years she'd been a creature of habit. Did what was expected of her and what she learned to expect of herself. When women's liberation came along that first time, she'd been too young to understand its power; in the sixties, she was a mother, somebody's wife. Still, like the spirit of a troubled soul she hovered on the edge of things, intrigued, tempted. Women could be brash and demanding and exciting. Something called to her in the sixties. She didn't answer, but she hadn't entirely forgotten the sound of that call. It had been the call of her childhood friends gathered beneath her bedroom window. "Emily! Come out! Come play in the woods."

She dried herself briskly with a thick white towel and stepped out of the tub. Her nightie was comforting. A statement. She slipped it over her head. She would not let on that she found him interesting. He'd touched her back just once, lightly, as they went out through the hotel doors into the parking lot to gather their luggage. It had been to guide her through, nothing more. But alarming little explosions had gone straight down through her vertebrae.

Jeronimo had expected Emily's sojourn in the bathroom to last longer than it did. Women had so many little things to attend to in bathrooms. He was never quite sure what things, only that it took an inordinate amount of time to do them. He'd been staring absently at an uninspired desert landscape hung over the bed when out she came, startling him with a little tra-la, "Your turn!" He grabbed up his pj's and fled into the bathroom.

There were little pools of water between the tub and bathmat, powder on the sink, the little intimacies of the bath. Disturbing, exciting. Women were mysterious and complicated, alluring and troublesome. You couldn't please them. They didn't know what they wanted, but they expected you to know all the same. Stubborn, too. The way she'd clung to that book! Fire could ignite spontaneously in those gray eyes when he was least expecting it. Was she expecting something of him? Could it be? Of course it could. And it was every bit his own fault. Climbing like some aged Romeo through her bedroom window.

Emily pulled the drapes. She slipped into the huge bed on the far side and lay on her back, hands clasped on her chest, staring at the ceiling. They would lay her out this way, she thought, soon enough. Her eyes would be closed (stuffed with something, she'd heard), nails buffed as they never were in life, and her hair would be blue.

She'd fought the hairdressers for the past twenty years, but who could fight the undertaker?

Well, who was she to complain? Let them do what they would. It was all for the living. To help them get on with things. She just wished it weren't such theater, such absurdist theater, the deceased prepped and primped like a holiday turkey. Yet she didn't like the idea of resting for the unforeseeable future in an urn on Alison's mantelpiece either.

Obviously she hadn't really thought enough about all this. Who would make all the decisions when the time came? It was terribly unfair to add to Alison's "to do" list. The least Emily herself could have chosen the pastor. But she knew only a rabbi, a sweet young man from her Italian class. Surely, when her time came, some rule or other would keep him from waving her Christian soul on. It was all such nonsense. If there was just the one God, why such a fuss about how to get to Him?

She plumped her pillows and sat up. Seven and a half hours from home and counting. How delicious it was to have become unpredictable. Now in the end she would at least have given them something to talk about besides her recipe for three bean soup and her volunteer work.

The shower droned on and on. How long did it take to scrub down? And what was she waiting for, anyway?

Emily dimmed the light by her side of the bed and thought about the way she would appear to Jeronimo when he came out of the bathroom. She grabbed a slick hotel magazine from the nightstand. Perhaps he would expect her to be sleeping. Perhaps that was why he was taking so long. But she had seen a spark of interest in his eyes, even on that first day. She was certain of that. What did one do at this age to fan the sparks? She had no idea. She was woefully lacking in experience with this sort of thing. Years ago when she'd admitted rather proudly that Alison's father had been her only love, Alison had been appalled. "Poor Mother!" she cried, as if Emily had been an impoverished child. She couldn't really counter with the truth. Despite his rather stiff demeanor, Frank had been a tender and attentive lover. With him, she'd plunged headlong into what she considered her rightful territory as a wedded woman. It was only in talking with close friends that she began to realize how far from the daily lives of most women that exotic territory was. Now, in her dotage, Frank's widow had run off with the first man who asked her. Emily could tell herself that it was her last chance. It was. She could say it had nothing to do with a man. Had her friend Sylvia come by with tickets for Hawaii, she'd have gone just as fast. There was little time left. Drowning, she'd have grabbed at whatever was thrown. But there was no dismissing the fact that Jeronimo, with his straight carriage and strong features, was a very attractive man. Taciturn, moody, temperamental, churlish, and occasionally downright rude, but, well, there it was. It was the very worst thing about women—the crazy belief that for you, and only for you, the sow's ear would turn somehow (one never knew quite how) into a silk purse. Too many fairy tales, that's what it was.

The bathroom door flew open. Out came Jeronimo in a cloud of steam and a pair of blue-striped pajamas. If he even noticed that Emily was in the bed, he didn't show it. Instead, he turned his back and slid his long legs under the covers. "Well, good night," he said and turned out his light.

"Good night, Mo," she said, reaching for hers.

The room was dark as the bowels of a mine. They each listened to the hum of the air conditioner, waiting for signs that the other had dropped off, she as far to her side of the bed as she could get and he just as far to his.

9

"Ah! Welcome to Sunnyrest. Welcome." The director came out from behind the reception desk, right hand extended, a quick little man wearing a liver-colored suit and floral tie. "Dave Davidson. And you are . . . ?"

Jeronimo shook the extended hand. "J. Martin Smith," he said. "And this is Mrs. Parsons. We're here to visit my brother, Lemuel Smith. Lieutenant Smith."

Dave Davidson's face fell. "A visit. Well, of course." Then his eyes lit up again. "But let me give you one of these." He reached behind him like a magician. "You know, just in case." Out came a brightly colored brochure. "Once you've seen the place—."

Something in Jeronimo's face seemed to steer him back on

course. "Ah, yes. Lemuel. You've come for a visit. Let me ring him up, tell him you're here." He dialed, then spoke into the phone. "Mr. Smith? Dave Davidson here. Your brother's come to visit. Your brother. Yes, yes. No, tall. Uh . . . gray hair? No . . . Here, let me put him on."

Jeronimo took the receiver. "Lem, it's me. Jay. Huh? I don't know. Twenty years, I guess. Thirty? Well, could be. Going to Yellowstone and you were, well, kind of on the way." Jeronimo's scowl deepened as he listened. After a while he said, "Well, do you want to see me or not?" Another pause. "Okay, then, we're coming up. Nope, didn't bring any cigars. Gave them up. Well, all right, then." He hung up the phone. "Hasn't changed a bit," he announced. "Ornery as ever. Just like the old man." Emily bit back a smile, but he caught her at it. "Runs in the family, I guess," he said sheepishly. "But he takes the cake. Wait'll you see."

Emily said she couldn't wait.

Emily had always been perplexed by the way men, particularly the older ones, greeted one another after long absence. So matter-of-factly, as if they'd spoken the previous day. "Lem," Jeronimo said, shaking the hand his brother stuck out.

"Jay," Lem said.

Once their hands had dropped away neither seemed to know what to do next. Then Jeronimo remembered his manners. He took a step backward, nudging Emily ahead of him like a small child. "This is Emily," he said. "Emily Parsons." He nodded his dome at one, then the other. "Emily, Lem."

"Pleased to meet you," Lem said, bowing over the hand she offered him. "Come on in, come on," he said and waved them through the door.

The small bedroom–sitting room was dimly lit and crammed with ornately carved mahogany furniture. Emily restrained herself from marching straight across the room to the window and yanking open the shade. Lem appeared to be preoccupied or perhaps a little disoriented. Emily thought he must be in shock from seeing his brother after all these years.

"Sit down, sit down," he ordered, indicating several possibilities upon which they could perch or lounge. Jeronimo dropped into a brown plaid recliner, one of a pair. Emily sat at a dining room table in the center of which was an arrangement of faded orange paper lilies.

Lem turned several times, in the way of a dog settling down for the night. Then he sat in a kind of angry huff in the second recliner. "So," he said. "So. What brings you here?"

Jeronimo's bushy eyebrows shot up. "Did I say something brought me? Just stopping by, that's all. See what you were up to."

"Well, you see it," Lem muttered. "If you're looking for a place to settle, this is as good as any. Better than some."

"Settle? Not on your life. We're on the road, Em and me. Aren't we, Em?"

"We certainly are," she agreed.

"Huh." Lem eyed Jeronimo with suspicion. Or derision. Emily couldn't tell which.

"Old folks' homes aren't for us," Jeronimo said. "Right, Em?"

She felt some sympathy for Jeronimo's brother, who seemed to diminish as Jeronimo spouted. "Well, Sunnyrest isn't an old folks' home, Mo. It's a—"

"Retirement community, you old futt." Lem shot a grateful glance at Emily, then glared at his brother again. "On the road, huh? A bum's life. I always knew how you'd end up. Just like the old man."

"Full of crap!" Jeronimo cried. "You're so full of it, just like always. You think this is the good life, don't you? Four walls and a crapper."

Emily sat back, horrified. How could brothers reunited after forty long years leap straight at each other's throats like a pair of hyenas? And yet she was amused to see how much the two men were alike, not so much in appearance but in so many of the little things. The way they sat, for instance, legs crossed, weight on the right hip and leaning forward aggressively, as if to snatch the words from the air the minute you spoke them. Lem had a ring of hair left and some extra pounds stashed around his middle, but he was nearly as tall as his older brother and had the same long neck and bones.

But there was something quite different, too, something that Emily couldn't put a finger on.

"How's the boy?"

"Fine," Jeronimo spat. "Fine. Couldn't be better." His fingers drummed the armrest.

"Married yet?"

"No, no." Jeronimo shook his head. "Well, you know how kids are."

"Kids?" Lem shot back. "Todd's, what? Must be pushing fifty."

"Forty-seven. Barely. That's young these days. Right, Em?" He didn't give her a chance to answer, barely glanced her way. "He's too busy for women, believe me. He's got too many irons in the fire. Women are the last thing on his mind." In his passion he'd worked up a sweat. He fidgeted in his seat, brushed lint off both knees of his trousers. He seemed helpless in his search for some way to redirect the conversation. "Where's Shirley, anyway?" he cried at last, leaping blindly onto the back of a new horse. He mopped his face with his handkerchief. "Hot in here," he muttered.

Lem frowned. He glanced at the window, then down at his hands. He sucked his teeth several times before answering. "Shirley's over t' the other side," he said at last.

"Over what side?" Jeronimo bolted up out of his chair. "You mean she's dead?"

"What? Oh, hell." Lem got up and stomped over to a small cart on which there were several bottles of liquor and water glasses. "No, she's not dead. *Jesus.*" He swiveled back to glare at Jeronimo. "Where's your sense? Where's your good sense? No, she's not dead. She's only over to the other side of this . . . place." He waved a hand in the air as if to pluck the right words out of it. "The what-do-you-call—convalescence side. Broke her hip." He splashed some whiskey into a water glass. "Well, she never did listen. What'll you have?"

Jeronimo said he'd have the same as his brother and sat back down. "Just a glass of water, please," Emily said. Lem returned with the drinks and dropped down across from Jeronimo once again. Emily calculated the room to be about the size of Alison's master bathroom. In it, along with the two large chairs, were a double bed, a highboy dresser, a bookcase filled with paperbacks, the dining set, and a rocking chair. On nearly every surface were dog figurines. A larger-than-life-sized portrait of a mixed breed hung over the bed. To break the uncomfortable silence Emily asked about it.

"Sergeant Bob," Lem said, his mournful eyes fixed on the portrait. "He's passed on. Some ten, twelve years. That's the polite way to say he's dead, but my brother here—"

"I'm sorry to hear about your wife's accident," Emily smoothly interrupted. "How did it happen?"

Lem told the story with many stops for sighing and for the sucking of his teeth. Emily began to see what was so different about the two brothers, whose basic temperament seemed so similar. Lem had given up. His shoulders sagged. Where Jeronimo's eyes were bright and filled with curiosity, Lem's had clouded over and lost their spark. Under Jeronimo's skin the blood still boiled, but Lem's was prematurely clotted. What temper had been called up in him seemed merely occasional, because seeing his brother had resurrected old grief and unresolved quarrels.

"You can go on over there and see her if you want to," Lem said. "She won't talk to me no more. Says I tricked her into coming here in the first place."

When they'd come down the hall following Dave Davidson to Lem's room, all the doors had been closed. It had looked to Emily like a hospital corridor. The walls were pale green, without a single painting to relieve the dull sameness. When Jeronimo had suggested they stop to visit his brother at a place called Sunnyrest, Emily for some reason or other had registered only the "sunny" part. She'd pictured bright little cottages with yellow trim and rose gardens. But clearly it was the "rest" part that the place was in the business of providing. For example, Lem's bedroom slippers, a pair of dark green corduroy scuffs, though it was the middle of the afternoon. The place was depressing, a kind of holding tank, it seemed. She shuddered and hoped they'd leave soon.

"Staying for dinner?" Lem said. "You can if you want. We get guest passes." He frowned. "What's this? Thursday? It'll be meat. They usually serve some kind of meat on Thursday. Good day to stay for dinner. And there's bingo after."

He got up, gathered the two highball glasses, and took them over to the cart for refilling. Emily, with a look, conveyed to Jeronimo that she'd rather not stay for dinner. Everything in her itched to leave. She half expected a net to drop out of the ceiling and capture them, like fugitives on a planet where everybody was young and healthy and, above all, productive. What right to just plain fun had they at their age? This was where they belonged, right here with all the other oldsters. Out of the way.

Lem came scuffing back and handed Jeronimo his replenished drink. "They got something going every night—ceramics, movies, you name it. Kids' choir last night from over to the high school.

They were good, too." He spoke in a monotone, like a bored tour director.

"We've got to get back on the road," Jeronimo said. "But we'll stop by and see Shirley before we leave." Jeronimo stood. "So. You like it here, huh?"

Lem frowned as if he were trying to remember something important, something that might have happened in another life. "What? Oh, yes. Hell, yes. Everything you could want. Everything taken care of. All you do is get up in the morning and get yourself dressed. Great life." He put all that he had into the end of his little speech, but it fell flat nonetheless. "Best thing we ever did was sell the house and invest here. Don't have to worry about another thing. We even got a plot in the back, you know for when . . . Well, we all gotta go sometime, right, Emily?"

"Indeed we do." She had been thinking that she should call the children.

"How you gonna go?" he asked, leaning toward Emily as if to learn some valuable inside information. "By land or by sea? Gonna let them bake you? Cast your ashes in the ocean from a helicopter? What?"

Jeronimo pushed his brother's arm roughly, sloshing the whiskey in his glass. "What are you talking about, you old fool? Can't wait for the end, is that it? Spend your time sitting around this . . . this *mausoleum* thinking morbid thoughts. Why don't you go play bingo or something?"

"Now, Jeronimo," Emily said, her voice like a restraining hand. "Your brother's not being morbid. He's simply being responsible."

She stood, turning to Lem. "And I commend you for it. It's simply the final decision, that's all, isn't it? After an entire lifetime of decisions, whether to do this thing or that, wear a hat or go bareheaded, eat broccoli or a good rare steak. Why, it must be rather a relief to have done with it, I should think. Particularly for a military officer like yourself." Lem stood a bit straighter. The look in his eye said he thought this woman had a lot of sense and, if so, what was she doing with a goof-off like his brother?

"Well, you two ghouls can do what you like." Jeronimo got to his feet. "Sit and knit your damned shrouds. I'm going over to see Shirl. You coming?"

They went down several dim hallways, Lem leading the way. An occasional open door allowed a glimpse of a small, usually tidy room. In one, a tiny plucked thing had dozed off in a rocking chair. Her head lolled sideways, and her mouth worked as if finishing a speech begun some years before. A calendar with a tropical motif hung over the dresser. Each room they passed attested to some valiant attempt to personalize. Some had flounces and priscilla sheers at the window, some were filled with family pictures. All had the same air of forced cheer about them.

They turned a corner and passed a recreation room. Inside, a half dozen whiteheads led by a blond child-woman in a fuschia leotard waved their arms to the strident beat of disco music. "Like trees," the girl-woman cried. "Wave them like trees! That's it! You've got it!"

Shirley was asleep, her eyes sunk into deeply wrinkled purplish hollows. She looked more like a sick baby bird than the woman Jeronimo had described. By the side of the bed, along with the remains of lunch—green Jell-O, a slice of dry white toast—was a contraption with wheels on it for walking. "They made her get right up and push that thing around, right after the operation," Lem said. "It was terrible. I couldn't watch."

Someone on the other side of the curtain was working hard at breathing, a terrible ragged wet sound.

Shirley's eyes blinked open. "What are you doing here?" she said directly at Lem. "Roll me up."

Lem cranked the bed.

"Remember me, Shirley? Jeronimo."

"Of course I remember you, dear," she said, offering a sallow cheek for him to kiss. "I haven't lost my senses. It's just my hip. And who is this? Not Louise."

"Not a chance," Jeronimo crowed. "Couldn't get her on the road, so I left her. Naw," he admitted, "that's not exactly it. Louise *passed on*"—he glared maliciously at his brother—"some years ago. This is Mrs. Parsons. Emily Parsons. Met her in the library. How about that?"

Shirley chuckled. "Good for you. It's nice to meet you, Emily. Jay's needed a good woman. On the road, you say? Hear that, Lem? Now that's just what I wanted to do." She frowned, smoothed a trembling hand across the folded-over sheet. Looking up again, she said, "Have you seen those pretty silver trailers? The round ones? Well, I had my heart set on one. But then we saw this place."

She frowned and changed direction, obviously for the benefit of her new visitors. "Jay, you look wonderful. Doesn't he, Lem? My, how the time goes." She winced as she attempted to change positions in the bed. Jeronimo reached to help, his big hands cradling her shoulders. "For two cents, I'd go with you two," Shirley said. "I would!" She gasped and then began to weep.

"I'll get the nurse," Lem said and was out of the room like a shot.

Emily sat on the edge of the bed. "What can we do for you, Shirley?"

The frail woman blew her nose several times and shook her head. "I'm sorry," she said. "I'm not myself."

"Well, of course not," said Jeronimo. "How can you be? You've had an accident. Happens all the time, doesn't it, Emily? But you can't let it get you down, Shirley. That's the thing. Let your guard down and the bastards are right behind you with the . . ." He was going to say "coffin." And then "mop." "Well, the thing is not to give in. You're not a quitter, Shirley. Show 'em what you've got!"

Emily touched Jeronimo's hand to slow him down. His reaction to Shirley's distress was distress of his own. In that, he'd been quite similar to his brother, who had bolted from the room the minute his wife began to weep. They each wanted to take care of things. Neither could stand to see her cry. They wanted her fixed, and right away. But too often people couldn't so easily be fixed. Shirley would mend in her time, or perhaps she wouldn't. There was that to consider also, to look squarely in the face. Perhaps she would never leave her bed again. But flinching from things didn't make them disappear, and neither did blustering on about them. What Shirley needed was some plain and simple TLC.

Lem came back with a nurse. "Why don't we leave Mrs. Smith alone for a while?" the nurse said. "Is that what you want, Mrs. Smith? I've got your medication right here. Give me your arm. That's a girl."

Emily glared at the nurse. "She's not a girl," she wanted to cry, but Shirley was in enough distress without her adding to it. Was it all a plot? Why else did they all—nurses, doctors, bag boys, and bankers—try to turn you into helpless children the very second you stumbled? In that at least, Jeronimo was right. You had to watch your back, right up to the end. And perhaps, she thought, remembering her intended instructions about the blue hair, perhaps even after that.

"They ought to just shoot her." Jeronimo slammed the truck door.

"Mo!"

"Well, they should. As a kindness. The way you put a good horse out of its misery."

When he cranked the key and the engine growled into life, Emily felt life flooding back into her own body. By the way Jeronimo backed quickly out of the visitors' parking lot, Emily sensed he felt it too.

The place really did look dreary. Even the pink hibiscus lining the walk drooped. "Shirley will be fine," she said to reassure Jeronimo, though she wasn't at all convinced. Shirley wasn't living a life she'd chosen for herself. What incentive did she have for getting well? "Why, people live absolutely normal lives after hip replacement . . ."

"You call that normal? The life those two are living? I'd rather be dead."

"Well, now . . ."

"I would. Wouldn't you? Spend your Thursday nights playing bingo. Doing your little happy tree dance. It's humiliating. Makes me glad I finally got up off my ass and headed out."

"And got me on the way? Are you glad about that too?" There. She'd said it. So little of any real substance had passed between them, and it was all so strange. They needed a bit more to go on, didn't they, if they were to truly share this little adventure?

His eyes went momentarily from the road to her eyes. She saw, or thought she saw, a dozen thoughts cross his mind, things he might not ever tell her if she didn't ask. "Wouldn't have done it if I hadn't wanted you along," he said.

"You didn't answer my question. I asked if you were glad to have me with you."

He grinned. It was a lopsided grin, a wobbly grin, half of himself holding back. "I have to answer that?"

Emily saw the boy in him then, the one that never quite disappeared. His grin went straight to her heart, but she wouldn't back down. "Yes, you do."

"Well, I am," he said.

"Am what?"

"You're pushing me, Emily. Why are you pushing me?" His eyebrows came down, but she wouldn't be intimidated.

"Because you need it," she said.

"I do?"

"Yes."

He threw his head back and laughed so hard she thought he'd crack a rib. It was like throwing open a window, that laugh, letting air and light into a closet. "Emily," he said, "we're going to have a good time, you and me. We're going to sleep out under the stars, chase buffaloes, shed the years like a snake sheds its skin." He reached over and squeezed her hand, once, fast.

She squeezed back and kept his hand in her own.

"God, how can people live like that? All cooped up? I guess some don't have a choice, but the rest?"

"We'll send Lem and Shirley lots of postcards," Emily said.

Jeronimo shook his head. "That senile old fool."

"We'll lure them out of hiding," Emily said. "That's what they're doing, you know. I was doing the same thing at Alison's. It was safe. I was useful."

"At least you were useful. I was keeping the lawn trimmed."

She laughed, then continued her musing. "What makes us think that at some certain time in life—sixty-five, seventy-two, eighty—we've got to do a final settling down? That we've got to coast to the finish? I'm tired of coasting, Mo."

"You said it, babe."

"Babe? Huh! Babe. Well." She didn't know whether to be insulted or flattered. She chose the latter. She'd never been a babe before, but she was sure babes had lots of fun. "It doesn't matter how long we have, does it? What matters is that we savor every moment. Oh, I know that sounds like a cliché." Her stomach grumbled. She hadn't been able to hold down her breakfast again. Perhaps she'd do better with lunch. Some soup, maybe. Or some nice green flaccid Jell-O and dry white toast. "It's funny, isn't it, how all the clichés come true in time."

"We're going to live forever," Jeronimo said. "Starting now. First one over the finish line is a rotten egg."

At the entrance to the freeway he goosed the Ford and they rocketed north once again.

"Well, forever's a relative thing, isn't it?" Where sky met sand the horizon was a straight unbroken line. Emily put her face to the wind and closed her eyes. "Or is that another cliché?"

10

Emily put a quarter into the slot of the pay telephone, pushed the 1 button as Jeronimo instructed, Alison's number, and after a chiming sound and instructions, the number on Jeronimo's telephone card. It was, as he said, a whole lot better than feeding the machine coin after coin. *I'll have to get one of these,* she thought.

And then: *Why?*

Funny how the little things brought one up short. In Provo, where they'd stopped for breakfast, Jeronimo had wanted to buy Emily a pair of hiking boots. The pair he chose were quite lovely, considering their bulk, with bright yellow laces and soft, supple leather the color of pecans. She'd been terribly tempted, shoes being her particular weakness. But her mind kept drawing her eyes to the boots' black tread, substantial as truck tires. To wear it down would take a lifetime, a lifetime she didn't have.

She held out admirably, considering how much she really wanted the boots. First she insisted that her black lace-ups with the thick rubber soles were perfectly suitable for hiking. The salesman and Jeronimo exchanged a look that men all over the globe used as a kind of shorthand: Women, it said. What can you do with them? Then she said that her heels were particularly narrow, which was true. Boots had never fit her properly.

"Ah, but these," the salesman said and, like Cinderella's slipper, the boot was on her foot. They were irresistible.

As TC answered the telephone, Emily was scuffing the toes of her glorious boots through the dirt, determined to give them the beating they deserved for as long as she was able.

"Hello, Nana," TC said, as if he'd just seen her at breakfast. "Hey, Nana! Guess what? Our team won the soccer tournament. Isn't that cool?"

"That's wonderful, darling. And how is school?" A gasoline tanker rumbled past, sending swirls of dust into the open door of the glass booth. Emily pulled the door shut.

"Aw, school sucks. When are you coming back? Ma's pissed at you."

"Yes, of course she's upset. Did you get my postcards? From Las Vegas?"

"Nope," he said. Did she get me some dice? Some real dice?

"No dice," she said, and laughed. Then she said she would look for something in the woods where they were going next. TC suggested a stuffed owl. She said that was certainly an idea. Then she asked to talk to Sam and then Alison, in that order. TC dropped the phone and hollered for his sister.

Emily watched Jeronimo in the adjoining booth. The receiver was in his right hand, halfway to his ear, and he had the most vacant look on his face. It was obvious that he hadn't wanted to call his son. He seemed to be doing it only for her, which made no sense.

Samantha lurched straight into her agenda. There was a fundraiser at school for which Emily must make her Black Forest Cherry Cake. The ballet recital for which she'd worked so, so hard was Saturday afternoon. And Sissy the mouse had escaped again. No one but Emily could ever find her. "Nana, I need you to *be* here" was Sam's culminating wail.

Emily could picture the child's flushed face, the way she pursed her lips when distraught. "Do you, darling? That's lovely."

"Well, are you coming home, then?"

"Soon," she said.

"When, Nana? I need to know when."

"You'll have to be patient, Sam."

"It's very hard for me to be patient, Nana."

"I know it is, my darling, but try your best. It gets easier, the more you try. Now put your mother on, please."

Alison had apparently been waiting her turn. "Mother," she barked into the receiver. "Where the hell are you? What in the world have you done? Have you lost your mind?"

Emily sighed. "Alison, why do you suppose it is that every time one does something somebody else doesn't want one to do, one is accused of losing one's mind? Doesn't that seem, I don't know, a little off base? I'm not losing my mind, Alison. I'm having a perfectly lovely time. We're on our way to Yellowstone."

"We? Who's we? Mother, who are you with?"

"I'm with a very nice man. A gentleman," she added, stretching the truth just a tad. "Someone I met recently in the library. I told you about him. He cut our grass."

"You're with a man? A *man?*"

"Yes, Alison. A man. They're the other half of the species, darling. The ones with weaker social skills and less hair." Exceptions abounded on both counts, of course, but Emily wasn't in the mood to be charitable. Alison had put her on the defensive.

"I can't believe you're doing this. Are you sure you're all right? I can't believe this." Alison carried on and on until Emily said she'd have to go, that she was tying up a telephone someone might need. She said she missed them all. She said not to worry. She said she was having the time of her life.

Only later did it occur to her that, of course, they'd have expected her all along to have had the time of her life with them.

Jeronimo called Information. That was the easy part. There was no listing for a Todd Smith. He hung the receiver on its hook and turned away, swung open the door and turned back again. Emily would expect him to have done more than that to find his son. Staring absently at the dialing instructions, he recalled, though he'd sworn not to, the name of Todd's lover and then, remembering the trombones, he had the number in his head: 415-776-7676.

Maybe he wasn't slipping so badly after all, but why did he remember so perfectly only those things he didn't want to remember?

He'd tell her he tried. That Todd was out. He'd try again another time. Maybe Todd wouldn't be at "Jimmy's" house anyway. Maybe they hadn't patched things up as Todd had hoped they would. Maybe Jeronimo would not be able to find his son, even if he made a concerted try. It hadn't occurred to him until this moment that he might not be able to find his son if he needed to. His heart was knocking hard against his rib cage, he didn't know why. It was just his son, for God's sake.

There was nothing rosy about Rosie's Café. Emily chose a booth in the back, away from a table of smokers. Thinking of Alison, Alison's chaotic life, she absently dusted crumbs from the surface of a faded green-and-white-plastic tablecloth. A stuffed weasel stared with beady black eyes from a shelf above their heads. "We can go somewhere else," Jeronimo offered, but Emily said the place was fine, that she wasn't very hungry anyway.

He didn't see how she could survive on what passed her lips, a cracker or two, a cup of soup or tea. "Well, they've got the usual," he said, scanning a menu block-printed and encased in cracked plastic. "Burgers, sandwiches." He decided on a club sandwich and pushed his menu to the far side of the table so the waitress would see they were ready. But they weren't. Emily was still perusing her menu, frowning at it as if it were printed in Chinese. "What'll you have?" he said. He didn't want to push her, but women always took so damned long if you didn't push a little. "Have the fish plate. I'll bet it's good."

She closed the menu at last and rested her hands in her lap.

"Well?" he said.

"Well, what?"

"What are you going to have?"

"Oh, I don't know. The soup, I suppose. Anything but split pea. I can't abide green soup for some reason."

"You can't just have soup. Have the fish." Jeronimo lined up his utensils, fork on the left, spoon and knife on the right. "It'll be dinner by the time they get around to taking our order."

The waitress appeared at last, a desultory gum-chewing adolescent, and Emily asked her what soups they had.

"You've got to eat something else," Jeronimo said. "Something solid. Get a sandwich." He ordered his sandwich and a cup of coffee. "And bring her one, too," he said. "Another club sandwich."

Emily pursed her lips but said nothing. This time. But he was going to learn not to make decisions for her. And he would have to learn it soon.

When their sandwiches arrived, he watched as she nibbled at the edges of hers. She saw that he was watching and took a good-sized bite and lay the quarter-sandwich back on her plate. "That's quite good, isn't it?" she said, but perspiration had broken out on her forehead and on her upper lip. Her eyes looked overbright, as a child's with a fever.

"Are you all right?" He sounded more bothered than concerned, but he just didn't know how to let someone know he cared without simpering. To his way of thinking simpering was worse than not saying anything at all.

"What? Oh. Yes, I'm fine." Her smile was unconvincing. When she left to use the restroom for the second time—she'd already used it to wash her hands when they came in—he found himself staring at her uneaten sandwich and wondering if she was up to a trip like this. She didn't seem at all hardy. What he'd read as strength was mostly internal, her spirit, that and the way she carried herself.

She took several kinds of medication. He'd noticed the bottles that morning when she left her fat bag open on the seat of the truck. Couldn't see what they were for, but he himself took half a dozen different things at various times. Probably nothing serious. But he wished she'd eat more. He didn't like having to worry about people. And yet he couldn't help himself, Todd never far from his mind, a wound refusing to heal.

She napped after lunch, her head riding light against his shoulder. He liked the way her hair smelled. He wasn't used to that either. To smelling women. After a while she awoke and asked if he'd like her to read to him. Before he could think to answer, she was rummaging through her purse. Out came the small green bag he'd recognized from the day they had their first coffee. "Don't tell me," he said. "It's Yeats, isn't it? In French."

"Why, yes, yes it is. After our little coffee, our *date*"—her eyes were merry and she was blushing like a girl—"I went right out and bought this. I wanted to read Yeats and think of you the whole time. Does that surprise you?"

"Surprise me? I'm floored. After I dumped the table and fought with you over the check?"

"I may have to ask you how to pronounce some words," she said, opening the cover of the paperback and pressing it back. "It's been a while."

His throat constricted. "You're going to read that?"

"Well, only if you'd like me to."

"No!" he yelped involuntarily. When she turned startled eyes on him, he muttered, "Aw, Em, I don't know French. Never did. I just couldn't admit it that day when you asked me."

She laid her head back against the seat and laughed. "Well," she said, "that's a relief. I was going to do my best to impress you, but my accent is terrible, *tres* terrible. Full professors have wept in despair over it."

"You can read something else," he said. "I know. Hemingway. Everybody loves Hemingway, right?"

Before she could answer, he'd stopped the truck, leapt out, and retrieved a book from the camper. Emily took the worn paperback from him. *In Our Time*, said the title on the tattered green-and-brown cover. Below that, in black letters three times the size of the title, was the famous author's name. And beneath the famous name was a crude sketch in what looked to be brown chalk. It was of two indistinct figures in a rowboat about to set off upon a lurid green lake.

It occurred to Jeronimo with a kind of dull surprise that in the entirety of his overlong life, he'd never been read to. Every child he'd ever known had been read to at some time or another. Nowadays it was practically mandatory. Louise had read to Todd every night before bed, in fact much beyond the age when Jeronimo thought the boy should be reading to himself. In the midst of his own reading, he would hear the soft hum of her voice from Todd's room and feel strangely resentful, left out. Why hadn't he read to his son? With his love of books, you'd have thought . . .

She said she'd begin with "Indian Camp." He said it was his favorite. She had a fine reading voice. Hemingway had to sound like, well, Hemingway, and this she managed. Jeronimo had read the Nick Adams stories many times, and the images his mind made over the years came hurtling back: Nick on the river with his father, that perfect harmony between man and boy, between men and the river and the fish, broken only by an occasional word, and then only if absolutely necessary, absolutely right.

Of course he'd pictured Nick's father as his own, and over the years that fictional father had completely effaced the original. (How many fathers he had created in the absence of the one who'd instigated his birth.) And Jeronimo had taken on himself what he could of Nick. The stiff upper lip, the refusal to feel any but the toughest blows.

Now it occurred to him that he would get a fishing rod for Emily. The couples he'd seen fishing together by the side of the road had always made him want the same for himself and Louise, but fish came out of a box for Louise, in pieces, coated with crumbs. Or did he just imagine that? Maybe he'd never asked her to come along in the first place.

"Dark story, isn't it?" said Emily, closing the book. But she'd read the story so well, he was certain she felt for it the same admiration he did. It was Hemingway, after all.

Jeronimo was filled suddenly with a sense of well-being, of absolute rightness. To what did he owe this second chance? Did he dare trust it? In this life colors were brighter, edges were sharper. People seemed to have lost their general nastiness. How could that be? He himself seemed to be riding higher and lighter in the saddle.

Was it love? How could it be? He was too old to fall in love. This, what he felt with her, was something better, less frantic, wiser. She matched him in ways he'd never expected and didn't fully understand. She had become, almost overnight, a necessary part of his life. Her voice was now woven into his stories. It was as if she'd always been there. The old codger creaking away his life in the green corduroy recliner with his deep-seated fear of dying alone seemed another person, some other Jeronimo. It seemed now as the old truck pushed toward the great wilderness that he might never die, but that if he did someone would be there. He wouldn't be mumbling his final words—he wondered idly what they'd be. A request for water? A curse?—in an empty house of empty rooms.

In this feeling of expansive well-being, he reached over and patted Emily's thigh. She smiled up at him over her reading glasses, her gray eyes speculative. But he needn't tell her, he reassured himself, what he'd been thinking—never told anyone how morbidly afraid he'd been of breathing his last all alone, never would. She seemed to know things without having them all spelled out. Women's intuition. He'd always set great store by that. She was the perfect woman for him, the perfect partner.

11

Emily had swallowed an extra capsule in the ladies' room at Rosie's Café, but the pain persisted, a droning, demanding presence. The story had done little to distract her, though it was better than most Hemingway stories she'd read. The boy, Nick, had promise, but it was clear that he would eventually emulate the father, who, given every opportunity for the deepest father-son intimacy, said only the most enigmatic and useless things. Romantic foolishness of the worst kind. The idea that if one were completely in tune with nature and one's fellow beings, words were extraneous, impediments actually.

When Jeronimo patted her thigh, she thought about the long exploratory conversations they would have around the campfire. She stuffed the Hemingway between the seat and the door. Thank goodness Jeronimo had brought other books.

They had been climbing for some time and were driving now through high country. Joshua trees and scrub gave way to lob-lolly pine and then finally the real thing, trees that grew straight into the clear blue sky. Emily gazed up through the windshield into the trees, their branches interlaced with shafts of brilliant late-afternoon sunlight and, beyond, bright clouds. "I think we've found it, Mo," she said.

"Hmmm?"

"Heaven," she said.

"Then we'd better stop for the night," he said, humoring her.

She said very solemnly that that was just the right thing to do.

They turned into a campground and followed the winding, narrow road to a spot by the lake gleaming silver between the trees. Jeronimo parked and reparked the camper several times, pulling out and backing up until he had it just right. "Can't sleep if it isn't level," he said. Jeronimo made a big deal about showing Emily everything, from a carton of oatmeal to a set of metric wrenches, all in their proper places. "Good solid mattress," he said, thumping the bed but avoiding her eyes.

"And this looks quite comfortable," she said at once, indicating the red plastic bench seat. "This will do quite nicely for me."

Jeronimo pretended to fuss. He insisted that she take the cab-over bed, that no one could possibly sleep on "that bench thing." But then, of course, it occurred to both of them that if she, barely five feet tall, couldn't sleep on the bench thing, how could he? And if she were in the double bed and he couldn't sleep on the bench thing, where would he sleep? Well, of course he must take the bed, she said. She'd be fine on the "couch." They couldn't quite bring themselves to look at the double bed as they settled the issue and went back outside.

Jeronimo took down the two bright blue folding chairs he'd bought in St. George and attached with bungee cords to the aluminum ladder. With great deliberation he set them just so, side by side facing the fire pit. Satisfied, he gazed from fire pit to his old red camper and then at last, almost shyly, to Emily. "Well," he said, "that's that."

As the sun began to set, they strolled down to the lake. When Jeronimo grabbed clumsily for Emily's hand and tucked it around his bent arm, she nearly laughed. But then she remembered that it was she who had taken his arm in just this way, straight out of another century, in the library.

Jenny Lake. Who had it been named for? Some pioneering woman, she hoped, some brave soul ahead of her time, the first to come upon the lake in all its pristine beauty. But it was probably named for the wife of some pompous politician.

A pair of ducks paddled past, and Emily thought about saying that the mallard with its brilliant green breast and his dowdy little wife reminded her of herself and Jeronimo. But it wasn't true, a silly thing. Her arm was snugly threaded through Jeronimo's arm, and for a moment—for just a moment—she felt like weeping. But that, too, passed.

A cold wind came in with the sunset. "We'd better have a fire," Jeronimo said. He dropped her arm abruptly.

Emily watched Jeronimo march off in search of kindling. She

felt a little—what was it? Abandoned. Yes. Dropped off, somehow. A pioneer wife told to stay behind in the fort while the men went off to hunt. Then she told herself she was being silly and began instead to search for something wifely to do. There was only so much you could change in a man this age. And did she really want to stomp through the woods in search of broken branches?

Jeronimo returned and dumped his armload of kindling next to the fire pit. He didn't seem to notice the blue-checkered cloth she'd spread on the rough wooden table, nor the jay's feather and sprig of pine stuck in the water glass. She could see as he began to prepare the fire that he had gone into himself, that she and the rest of the world had for the moment been set aside.

How easily he became his own company. For her it had always been difficult. She was like a stubborn old violin tuned to a single song. Children's cries, mealtimes, laundry cycles. How easy it had been to fall back into all that after Frank passed on and Alison sent up her cry for help. She had been relieved even. No longer would she have to invent a life, take up decoupage, pen in her social calendar weeks in advance, adopt a Welsh corgi.

She didn't have to go in search of herself either. It was far easier not to. All she had to do was sell her home, pack her bags, and a life would be there to meet her at the Santa Barbara airport, ready-made.

She watched Jeronimo as he built his fire. All of his movements were interconnected, as if he knew each one beforehand. Certain pieces of wood belonged in certain places, laid at certain angles. He hummed as he worked, something light and tuneless.

The sky was clear and black, dotted with stars. Cooking fires blazed in other campsites, seemingly suspended in black space on all sides. Children called to one another through the trees. A woman laughed deep in her belly. Someone strummed a guitar. Jeronimo lit a match, touched it in several places to bits of dry twig and paper. His face blazed up in the light. In that moment, he looked vulnerable, defenseless, and Emily's heart caught with the sudden realization of all she had been expecting of him, simply because he was a man. She had not been fair. She had held back. She had not, as he might put it, laid all her cards on the table. She had not told him the single most important thing.

Her feeling of delighted well-being left her, went up in the smoke above Jeronimo's fire.

Emily did her best with the steak, a slab of blackened flesh she'd not have touched in the best of circumstances. She nudged it around the paper plate while he dove into his, recalling between bites years of frozen dinners and greasy Chinese takeout.

He went to the fire and returned with two charred potatoes. He dumped one on her plate, though she'd already twice refused it. "Eat," he demanded. "Eat." Jabbing at the potato—at her?—with the tines of his plastic fork.

"Now, this," Emily said at last, dropping her napkin onto her plate, "this is going to have to stop."

Jeronimo looked up from his feast, bewildered, his fork and knife suspended above paper plate and raw red meat.

"I won't have you making my decisions," she said. "I'm far

too old for that. It's humiliating. I'd have never come along if I'd thought you had such little respect for what I decide."

He looked at her wide-eyed, unable to swallow his half-chewed chunk of meat, unable to speak.

"Oh, I know you think you've my best interests at heart. Everyone thinks they have my best interests at heart. Seventy-nine years of life and I'm still not trusted to know what I want." She felt herself heating up.

"Seventy-eight," he muttered when his mouth was free. "You said you were seventy-eight."

"Whatever." She waved him away with the back of her hand.

"You're not?"

"What?"

"Seventy-eight."

"What does it matter how old I am? Haven't you been listening at all?"

"Well, sure. I just thought you were seventy-eight, that's all."

"Have you heard one thing I've said?"

"I said I did."

"What, then?"

"Huh?"

"What did I say?"

"Well, you said I shouldn't tell you what to eat anymore."

"You know that's not all." She pinched her mouth at him. "You know that's not all. Don't you, Jeronimo?"

He frowned. He shuffled his boots. "Are we through now?"

She thought he meant with the meal. "Through? Well, yes. I am. I certainly don't intend to eat that potato."

"No, I mean fighting. Are we through fighting?" Jeronimo was unnaturally subdued. Mulish. A four-year-old made to stand in the corner.

"We're not fighting," said Emily. "We're having a discussion. We're laying down the ground rules."

He pushed away the most prized bites of fat-encased meat that he'd saved for last. "Ground rules," he repeated. She couldn't tell what he was thinking, and she didn't much care that she'd hurt his feelings.

They tidied up the campsite without meeting eyes, each caught up in separate tasks, in the bruised self-righteous aftermath of their first quarrel. She left the greasy pan and spatula for him.

"Well, I won't," Jeronimo said after a time. Emily had moved on to other things. She'd been thinking about Sam, about learning Spanish with Sam. Who would help Sam with her homework now? It took her a moment to come back. "I won't tell you what to do anymore. I mean it. It's a bad habit of mine. Todd said the same thing." He scratched the back of his ear. "But an old dog can learn new tricks, right?" He said this with such a heartfelt determined look on his face that she had to smile.

"Most certainly," she agreed. "Old dogs do the best tricks, I think. Once they catch on."

He went into the camper and came out with a bottle of Courvoisier and two tiny glasses. He filled them carefully as she watched.

"I was thinking about pioneer families," she said, "while you were out there gathering wood. It's as if we're here in the wilderness with all these other adventuresome families on our way to win the West. This is such fun, Mo. And to think, life might have gone on just as it was. Not so bad. But . . . *predictable*. Oatmeal days."

"Oatmeal days?"

"Well, you know what I mean. Bland. Ordinary. But now there's you. You're anything but ordinary, Mo. Extraordinary, I'd say."

"As in extraterrestrial?" Up went his eyebrows. "Like *out* there somewhere, right?" He plunked down in the chair next to hers and stretched out his long legs, boot soles to the fire. "Well, I'm used to that."

"To what? To being different?"

"Eccentric, weird, you name it. And getting worse with age."

"Perhaps just more . . . individual. Unique," she suggested. "That's a gift, isn't it? A gift of age. One can get away with so much more."

She reached for his hand and cradled it in her lap. "Look at all those stars, Mo," she said, tipping her head back. "Extraordinary, wouldn't you say? Each one absolutely unique. But to each other they probably look pretty much alike, don't you think? Just another dazzling face. Why, we'd have passed each other on the street and never said a word had it not been for Yeats."

"Yeats," he said, with little of the old reverence. His need for poetry, fantasy, had retreated somehow in the face of this real thing. Of Emily.

"Tell me all about your childhood, Mo. Begin with your earliest memory. I have to know everything."

The intensity in her voice startled him. The way he saw it, there wasn't much to tell and it wouldn't take long. They had all the time in the world for stories, if that's what she wanted.

"I don't remember much," he said. "There were never any photographs, things like that."

"Start with a picture in your mind," she said. "Start with one of those."

Jeronimo began with the mental photograph of his mother standing at the coal-burning stove. As he spoke, he stirred his fire, shifting the wood to keep it going, laying on another log. Emily stared into the fire and saw Jeronimo's life where it began, a life without words. It was no wonder he'd disappeared into books as soon as he discovered them. But he'd been a mischievous child until then, and his stories all had an invented Tom Sawyer ring to them. He said without a change of tone that he didn't remember the day his father left, only that he was gone for days, then weeks, before his mother told him anything. She was pregnant then with Lemuel and slept through her days, leaving Jeronimo to fend for himself.

After a while he wound down. "Well, that's about all I remember. Little boys are all about the same, I guess. Well, you had one, so you know."

"We didn't have him long enough," Emily said. "He never had a real boy's life. He was my baby. He was my baby until the end."

When had she last talked about Evan? One was expected to bury memories with the dead, at least all the sad memories. There was the requisite grace period—she didn't know exactly how long it was, only that it was never long enough—and then the box must be shut. She'd done her best to oblige, avoiding the mention of her dead son except on occasion to Frank. People didn't want to think about death. There were plans to be made, promotions to vie for, babies being born and growing out of their shoes. One looked ahead, always ahead.

"Death always nips you on the heels," Emily said into the stars. Jeronimo's hand encased in her two was warm and rough and alive. "But, really, when you turn around you see that it was there all along. Our Evan had leukemia. There was no cure then. I went a little crazy. Fed him carrots until he turned orange. Took him to a faith healer. But he withered away before my eyes. In the end he just curled into himself, all tiny bones and blue veins, skin like parchment. He died in my arms."

She didn't say how hard she'd fought to keep him, how they'd had to pry her arms away in the end. All the same, the tears flowed. She noticed now that each time she'd cried over Evan, the tears were somehow different, even a different consistency, viscous. She didn't know how that could be, only that they were. Life went on. There was no stopping it. You changed with your grief. This time she wept for old losses and for losses to come, and yet she was not sad. How could she be? Life in this moment was as rich and full of promise as it always had been.

"Jeronimo?"

"Mmmm?" He'd wanted to shrink away from her sadness.

"They say there's a star in the sky for every person who's ever passed. Do you believe that?"

"Nope. Do you?"

"No, but I'd like to." She paused and then said firmly, "I think I shall."

Jeronimo resettled the coffeepot with his free hand. "You can't just start believing something just like that, Emily. Just because you decide to."

"No? Why not? Whoever said there had to be a lot of soul-searching and angst about it? Why can't one just choose to believe in something and have done with it?"

"Well, it's not . . . it's not right. Beliefs are serious things, Em. They run your life. They're engines, kind of, for action."

"All the more reason to change them when they no longer work. Or overhaul them, to keep with your metaphor."

She watched him bite down on that idea, swirl it around. She could tell he found it intriguing, though she knew he believed in his Puritan heart that nothing worthwhile came easy. Life was hard work, not miracles. You got what you paid for. He'd honed the edges of his spirit with worn-out beliefs, thinking them not only serviceable but original. She knew that about him without his ever having said it.

He frowned, shook his head. "Well, I suppose one could," he said, "choose to believe something."

The flames were low now, the fire settled within itself and glowing orange. With her tears Emily had opened a door, and through it she and Jeronimo walked hand in hand, trading one for one some of the confusions and resolutions of their long lives. Jeronimo saved Todd for last. He had lost a son, too, he said. Not in the way she had, but this grief was current and rubbed like a cheap shoe. "He turned out to be gay," he said. "Nobody's fault, I guess. They say you can't blame the mother anymore. It was better when I could do that, for some reason. Guess I didn't want to blame myself."

"And now you blame him."

From anyone else he'd have taken that as a rebuke, but Emily merely spoke aloud what was in his mind.

"Well, it's somebody's fault. Some P.E. teacher. *Somebody.*" Agitated, Jeronimo snatched back his hand and ran it several times over the dome of his head.

"Biology," Emily said. "Blame biology if you must. But it would be so much easier if blame weren't involved, my dear. There's so very much we don't know."

"I don't want to talk about this," Jeronimo said, and the mood shattered.

He slapped at an invisible mosquito. The fire crackled. At a distant campfire a dog barked.

"I mean, he's normal in every other way. He's a good-looking guy, for crying out loud, a nice guy. Heart right out there on his sleeve. He'd do anything for you. For anybody. Friends, strangers, doesn't matter. Smart, too. Top of his class. And you should hear the kid sing."

"I'd like to," she said.

"You never will. I told him this time . . . well, I said as long as he was going to live *that* way, I didn't want to have anything to do with him."

"Oh, dear."

"He just doesn't know where to draw the line. Told the mailman he was expecting a letter from his lover. His lover, *Jimmy.* The mailman, for Christ's sake. I've known the guy for years. Years! Now I just let him drop the mail in the box and go on."

"You'll have to try him again tomorrow," she said.

"Todd?"

"Well, surely not the mailman."

Emily took back Jeronimo's hand, turned it palm up and ran her finger down the long lifeline. She had fended off the growing realization as long as she could, but it came over her now with such force she could ignore it no longer: She should not have come. The decision to run off with a man she hardly knew, no matter how tough the sinews of his soul, was selfish and irresponsible. After a while, he would come to need her, and she would not be there.

She awoke covered with stars. Blinking herself awake, she saw that Jeronimo was not in his sleeping bag. Well, the idea to sleep out under the stars had been more romantic than practical. His idea, too, nurtured along by the extra nip or two of the Courvoisier.

Emily's back was stiff, but, mesmerized by stars more brilliant than any she could remember, she was reluctant to go to her skimpy plastic bed. She wanted to lie beside Jeronimo. She let the thought blossom fully in her mind. How surprising it was to admit how much she'd missed physical intimacy with a man. Widowhood had neutered her. She supposed it didn't have to, but it was easier somehow to let one's sexual self atrophy than to go out and do something about it. That, too, was expected. That, too, had to be put into the box and tucked away.

What would Alison have done if her eighty-year-old mother had taken a lover? Booted her out? The thought was delightful in its way. Alison needed some shaking up of her own beliefs, if not an overhaul. Or she'd end up with another snake like Hal. Emily shuddered, recalling the string of half-truths and outright lies traced back at last to the hole from which the man had crawled. And the children's father, Richard, had absolutely no substance. He was thin as nonfat milk. If she could wish on a star, Emily would wish a good man, a companion, for her daughter. Someone who loved her as she needed to be loved. It was all well and good to be a single woman; Emily had nothing against the independent life. It was an old-fashioned predilection, she supposed, but people were meant to couple, to shore each other up when times were hard—and they often were—to hold each other in the soul's dark nights.

Emily picked her way over the cold ground and climbed up into the camper. In the light of the tiny stove she could see the outline of Jeronimo in the bed. He lay on his back with his mouth open. She sat for a moment on the bench seat, thinking, collecting herself. Then she went up the ladder and climbed in beside him.

She was not at all sleepy. The night and the stars had stirred her senses, made her adventurous. She touched Jeronimo's smooth chest, felt it rise and fall with his breathing. He lay stiff and still, his breathing shallow. She wondered if he always slept on his back.

She never could. Her fingers traced a collarbone, lightly, then followed a thin line of hair to Jeronimo's navel and stopped, went a few inches further and stopped again. He hadn't a thing on, not a stitch. And then she just couldn't resist. Didn't see the sense of it. She took the warm, soft weight of him in her hand.

"Mo?"

"Mmmm?"

"Is it all right?"

"Oh, Lord, yes." He'd been awake all along, probably from the moment she climbed in beside him. The words came out of him cracked and leaking. "Yes," he breathed. Then, after a little while, he gently tugged her hand away. "Never mind," he said. "It doesn't work anymore."

"Oh, well," she said in the way one might remark on the weather or a preference for a certain kind of soap. "Here, help me off with this." She sat up and with his help struggled out of her flannel gown. "Let's just explore the territory for a while."

"Well, I can't . . . you know," he said. "Don't expect . . ."

"What I expect," she said, "is a thorough exploration, Captain Smith. East and west, north and south." Levity helped. She was terribly nervous.

His hand trembled as he touched her cheek, his long fingers searching out the hollows of her face, her sharp jaw, the long, brittle bones of her arms. He said her name several times in several ways, trying in vain to cast the things he had no words for. He said her name like a chant or a spell. She took his hand at last, because she felt his hesitation, his fear, and guided it over her soft, flattened breasts and down to where she was warmest. "Oh, Lord," she heard him cry softly from a long distance, while she arched herself into his hand and bloomed open, a dizzying almost forgotten climb and a dropping away, an aching reach and again a falling away. "Oh, Lord," he said again.

"I didn't take you for a religious man, Mo," she said when her body had come back to its accustomed state. The intensity with which she had responded to his touch astonished her, but she'd wasted little time wondering about it.

"I didn't used to be one," he said. "I may be now."

She fell into a deep, dreamless sleep, her head locked within his big hands and pressed against his knocking heart.

12

A week passed. They filled their days with all the normal little things of a life. They cooked together, played Scrabble, read to each other. But as night fell, neither could wait to go "exploring." All Jeronimo's parts were now in glorious working order.

Then, on the eighth day, floating up out of sleep, warm and muzzly, Emily knew at once that she was alone in the bunk. She opened her eyes, stared for a while at the mottled yellow fiberglass ceiling, then rolled over and parted the curtains to peer out the tiny window. Snow. A light dusting over everything, the table on which they'd eaten their previous night's meal—macaroni and cheese, unnaturally orange, sticky as classroom paste—the fire pit they'd huddled around as Jeronimo's fire blazed through the threat of a bitter-cold early evening.

No fire this morning, no coffeepot steaming. Emily's spirits sagged, and the promise of a good snow did little to lift them. Across the blue-gray glitter of the morning, a single set of size twelve footprints had gone straight off into the woods.

She dropped the curtain and sighed. She sighed again, this time with exasperation as she struggled with the nightgown that had wrapped itself twice around her body. Almost from the first, he'd teased her unmercifully about her flannel gowns. Called them "sacks" or "bags." "Aw, leave off that flannel bag, Emily," he'd say after that first foray into his bunk when she'd climbed in beside him. Naked, they would lock together like pieces of an ancient puzzle, and Emily would tumble again into the deep, dreamless sleep of a child.

But he'd not teased her about the gown last night, not with the temperature well below freezing. And there was the other thing, what he had refused to let her say, that had come between them until at last, as night fell and the cold locked in, they lay side by side but apart in the separate cocoons of themselves.

Emily sat up. She dropped her legs over the side of the bed. Propped up on her two thin arms, hands clutching the edge of the bunk, she found herself nursing a single clear thought: The pain had come to stay. Sometime in the last few days, like a homeless being wrapped in the skin of its possessions, pain had settled in some available space behind her ribs. There was little respite now. She could dull its edges, but no longer could she ignore it or hope against vain hope that turning her life on its head, as she had done with Jeronimo, could somehow deflect the disease from its intended course. It forced her attention. Just as surely as she did with Sam and her demands, she was to have a relationship with this thing.

She gazed down into the tiny space that had become a home. It was nothing more than a metal cave, really, the size of a generous closet. A turtle's shell. A nest. Through one of the small windows a white block of morning light illuminated the scratched red surface of the counter and side-by-side coffee cups, Jeronimo's huge brown mug, hers with the eagles on it, the one he'd bought her in the Tetons. Hanging beside the child-sized stove was a yellow-checkered pot holder she'd picked up somewhere along the way, and on the face of the tiny refrigerator was a card made to resemble a cross-stitched sampler:

Beauty is a gift of youth
Age a work of art.

Emily had made these little inroads into Jeronimo's too tidy life, some without his full consent—there were coupons for All-Bran and chicken noodle soup in the drawer, a grapefruit spoon and a tea strainer, little things no one thinks much about.

And she had done that greater thing, the one that worried her days with him now, that sin of omission.

Dangling her bare feet with the long blue veins and the yellowed, twisted toenails, she pictured an angry Jeronimo stomping off through the snow, blowing steam into clouds, tearing through the frigid morning air, cursing her, cursing his own foolishness for ever having taken up with her. Then she pictured a befuddled Jeronimo, climbing ever so quietly into his clothes, carefully locking the camper door before trudging off, hands deep in his pockets, mind gone deep into itself.

Which Jeronimo was out there in the snow? How much had he guessed? How much did he know? Though he could behave the fool, as he had that first day in the library, he was not one in fact. So much of his blustering was for show. Just like Old Faithful.

Entering Yellowstone Park days earlier, Jeronimo whistling at her side, his hand cupping hers on the seat between them, Emily had been enthralled with everything. So enthralled that at first she could not speak. It was too immense, presented too much for the eye and mind to assimilate. Great rolling clouds cast shadows on mountain peaks that went on and on into the distance; peaks descending into canyons, and canyons into rushing sparkling rivers. It was too much to put words around.

And then she began babbling and couldn't stop. "It's magnificent, Jeronimo," she heard herself say over and over again. "Gorgeous. Breathtaking." Finally, because there were only so many words, at least in her limited vocabulary, to equal the experience, and so few of them really did, she stopped trying to find them. She settled into an awed silence that seemed after all the most appropriate response. They'd driven on toward the point at which the pale blue sky and gray-brown earth met, the line at the end of the earth. And she didn't speak of that either, of the desire to go on and on, the line always just ahead and always out of reach.

Jeronimo had said nothing for miles, just grinned at her enjoyment and his brilliance in having produced it all. She allowed him that vanity, turning to him in delight at each new discovery and each time finding that his face had changed, grown younger, brighter, the whites of his eyes clear as a young man's, his forehead smooth. And then when he could contain himself no longer: "Didn't I tell you? Didn't I?"

But of course, he hadn't. He'd simply told her the one little story, the story of the bison dying alone in the snow.

There had been few other vehicles, and most had been going the other way, late-season tourists like themselves but who now would make their way back to California and Utah, Nevada and Washington. The park would close the following week and wait out the winter buried in snow. "Just in time," Jeronimo said as the ranger at the gate handed over a map and a warning about the weather, which Jeronimo barely heeded. "Can you beat that? What timing, huh?"

They'd driven as far as West Thumb, then turned onto the road that led them to Old Faithful just as the geyser erupted. Jeronimo stopped the truck in the middle of the road, gazing up, lost in the thunder and spectacle of thousands of gallons of scalding water, steaming and spewing, shooting itself at a winter sky almost as white as itself.

Emily got out of the truck and made her way toward the knot of people gathered around the geyser. What few there were looked like a small United Nations delegation—a Japanese couple, two women in saris and ski jackets, a family speaking Spanish, a solitary very tall and very black man who could have hailed from Philadelphia or Ghana or any of a number of places in between. Emily joined the others and soon was marveling alongside the "Japanese couple," second-generation American college students, and the black man, who turned out to be Jamaican. It had always been so natural, this drawing toward others, born of a curiosity that each of Emily's parents at various times in her life had unsuccessfully attempted to restrain. "Unladylike," her mother pronounced. "Dangerous," warned her father, when Emily was well past forty and presumably able to recognize her own bogeymen.

Jeronimo was not much better than her parents. After she'd struck up a conversation in the St. George Safeway with a produce man, he'd told her afterward that she'd kept the poor man from getting on with things, when in fact it was Jeronimo who wanted to get on with things and the produce man who'd kept the conversation going: His wife made a great campfire lasagna, right in the skillet and did Emily want the recipe? He could give his wife a call, wouldn't take a minute.

All her life Emily had found that people, not all of them of course but most, were eager to connect, to share what they knew, to satisfy their own curiosity, and didn't Jeronimo think so? Not Jeronimo. While she chatted with strangers, he stood off to the side, looking out at the scenery, scuffling his impatient feet.

But that was changing. She'd begun to draw him in. After they'd conversed for a brief time with another elderly couple or, once, a disorderly but entertaining pack of adolescents, Jeronimo came away chuckling, dissecting some point someone had made. And didn't he think people were just fascinating? Fascinating? Well, that was a bit strong. Interesting, yes. Some of them were interesting.

Of course she didn't point out to Jeronimo, to the emerging Jeronimo, that once he'd stepped into the conversational waters with strangers, what he found so interesting was himself. Because, great ham that he was, Jeronimo generally did most of the talking. But it was a start. The reason Jeronimo had been so lonely all the years since his wife passed on was not that he disliked people — in fact, he was just as likely to swing wildly in the opposite direction and praise to the skies the intelligence of someone Emily thought stuffy and pedantic. The reason for his solitary and disgruntled approach to life was shyness. It didn't take a psychologist to tell you that most curmudgeons were simply shy. They hadn't the courage to reach out to others, and so they disparaged them instead.

How sad, thought Emily, climbing down the ladder to step on the bit of cold linoleum between the counter and the single bunk. Steeling herself against the icy air, she dressed quickly in sweater and slacks, pulled on Jeronimo's red-and-black-checkered jacket and night watchman's cap, gathered up the coffeepot, and stepped out into the snow.

If anything, it was warmer outside the camper. She turned her face into a shaft of sunlight that streamed down through the upper reaches of snow-laden branches and closed her eyes.

Quiet. Quiet. And deep within that, a peace, an absolute stillness that both moved and frightened her. She wasn't ready. She didn't know what that meant exactly, being ready. Too much of who she was, who she had always been, was still moving forward, anticipating the next experience, greedy for life.

And yet, inside, the new thing that she must come to know, no friend, yet more intimate than a lover.

She made her way carefully through the snow, more carefully than she might have before spending that time with Shirley. It was the sticky sort of snow, perfect for building snowmen and helping elderly ladies balance themselves.

She wondered what Lem and Shirley would say about all this. When Shirley dreamed about hitting the road in a shiny silver trailer surely she didn't envision frosty mornings in a nearly deserted national park. As the cold seeped up through Emily's ankles, she wasn't sure there weren't better places to be. Despite the beauty of the park, she looked forward to moving on. But to where? And why? She thought about her dying, about the last days. She wondered if it made any difference where she was when the time actually came.

And just as suddenly she knew it did. That it could make more difference than she'd ever before realized.

She found a faucet on a pipe sticking out of the snow, but no water came out of it. She supposed it was frozen inside the pipes. She returned to the shelter of the camper with a pot full of snow and fingers so stiff she couldn't strike a match. She cupped and blew into her hands as she had as a child on the old pond just down the road from their farmhouse where she'd first learned to skate. She saw herself as she was then, a precocious little girl, turning figure eights over and over again until the cold aching of her fingers and toes forced her to rest. Skating was her life then, so important that she dreamed it night after night. Why was that? And how was it that something so vital could pass into something else, and that new something then become the meaning of life? For a time, it was horses, then the boy—what was his name? the little towhead whose front teeth never grew back in, two farms over. Was it all a trick after all? What had she learned from falling in and out of love with skating and music and places and people? Anything at all?

She measured coffee into the strainer and set the pot on the stove. At last she got the stove lit. When Jeronimo returned she'd have hot coffee for him. Then she would sit him down and make him listen.

A half dozen times the day before, she'd tried to tell him. And each time he'd found some way to evade her. Did she see that? he'd cry. His long finger would point somewhere off into a canyon: a pair of hawks gliding, or were they eagles? There were bald eagles in the park, did she know that? They'd almost gone extinct. And had she ever seen an osprey?

So she figured he had guessed. She supposed it wasn't all that hard to tell that something was wrong. He'd watched her pick at food, saw what was left on her plate. From time to time, the pain would clutch its stubborn fist just under her diaphragm and she would break into a cold sweat. There was no hiding the evidence.

And then there was the morning, Tuesday, when she'd left camp on some pretext or other and he'd found her doubled over, retching, a hand against the rough bark of a tree to steady herself.

How solid that tree had felt, how live the bark. It was as if she'd laid her hand on the shoulder of a trusted friend. She'd leaned against that tree until she was certain her legs would not give, remembering morning sickness, the shock of that, of a young woman's introduction to maternity. This of course was very different, the other end of things. No reward at the end for having endured. Release only, and then the thought that perhaps release would be its own reward.

Shaken, her face bathed in cold perspiration, she'd raised her head to see Jeronimo there beside her. He'd not said anything, just took out his handkerchief, shaking it to release the folds, and passed it to her. And, for the first time in their knowing one another, which seemed now half a lifetime, she'd avoided his eyes. "Must be a touch of the flu," she said. But the words had cost her. What she had all along allowed herself to call a sin of omission became a sin of commission. She knew then that she would have to go on with her dissembling or make an honest woman of herself. She chose the latter.

Raising her eagle cup of steaming black coffee to her lips, Emily resolved that the time for omissions and evasions was past. This wintry day when the whole world outside was quiescently accepting the inevitable, she and Jeronimo would have their talk. She would tell him about the cancer. She would use the right word. She would tell him she was sorry.

Sorry? But she wasn't, not really. If she'd told him to begin with, none of this would have been the same. They'd have talked death, not life. Instead of living, they'd have been preparing every minute for the end.

She wondered how long he would stay out in the cold before giving in.

She took up the Hemingway book and settled into a blanket to wait, but the story she began to read was really quite silly, about a woman who fell in love with a cat while her brand-new husband wandered about outside in the rain. She began to lose interest. And she could not have given it her full attention anyway, as she was listening with the more alert part of herself for Jeronimo's footsteps.

13

Jeronimo had gone much farther into the woods than he had intended. Intentions were flimsy things when the mind wasn't right. And his wasn't right. Sometime during the early morning—he couldn't tell what time it was—he'd awakened or been awakened abruptly, his heart thudding like someone breaking down a door. He lay very still, letting the thought seep in that the old ticker might be going, might at last be giving out. He took several deep breaths, willing the organ to calm itself. This was not the time or place to have a heart attack. Why he thought an act of will could chart the course of his heart, he didn't know. It just simply couldn't give out here. What would Emily do? She didn't even drive.

He laid his hand lightly on her hip, her bird bone of a hip, not to wake her but to calm himself, and at last his heartbeat slowed.

Not an attack after all. Something had frightened him in the night, that's all. A nightmare maybe, though he could not remember dreaming. It was as if something, a dark thought, had wormed its way into his heart before his mind got a grasp on it. His heart had got a preview, like those movie previews of coming attractions, and didn't like what it saw. She was dying. He didn't need the words from her to know that. Didn't want to hear them. Words made things once-and-for-all real.

A light snow had begun to fall as he went deeper into the woods. Fat, lazy flakes drifted through his vision, never good, and settled on his eyelashes. He blinked them off.

Somewhere near this place he had seen the bison with his father. He remembered the mountain range across the canyon at the edge of the woods, the peculiar shape of it and the upthrust fault at its western end. And he knew he would not find that one special place now, not after all these years. Why did he ever think he could locate a single small place in all this vast landscape? And why the hell did it matter anyway? He gave himself another of his mental kicks in the butt and turned to retrace his steps.

He knew that his father, could he see Jeronimo now, would be scoffing. He would ask him his purpose for having gone out into the snow, and Jeronimo would not know how to answer. All his life he'd tried to couple action and purpose as his father had always claimed to do, but all that was unraveling now. There were things you had no control over, things that had no purpose he could see. He felt like Job in the wilderness. Worse! Because he had no God to blame.

Something rustled in the bushes, and he turned quickly. Nothing. A chipmunk or marmot. There wasn't much above the ground. Animals were smarter than people. People did strange and foolish things, particularly when they were old and could no longer think straight.

He should have known. Should have seen she was not well all along. Why hadn't he at least entertained the possibility before taking up with her? Was he so caught up in those vibrant gray eyes that he'd not noticed at all the painfully thin wrists? How could he have been so blind when all his friends—well, he didn't have all that many, but when every last one of them was suffering some illness or malady or damn near dead, why did he think a woman her age would be as hale as he? What were the odds of that anyway? Thousand to one? Hundred thousand to one? He kicked at a pinecone.

Now he understood how it was that she'd gotten ready so fast that night in her bedroom. Her suitcase had already been packed. Not in expectation of going anywhere with him (she couldn't have guessed). Not for the trip to Montana, but for the inevitable stay in the hospital. Later. When the time came, she'd have been ready.

He could confront her with that. She wouldn't deny it. But what was the use?

He studied the faint outline of his own footprints marching toward him. *Coming and going,* he thought. *Coming and going. That's all I've been doing my whole life.* Just like some damned squirrel. Mindless. And with a whole lot less purpose. At least a squirrel knew what it had to do and why. He'd never known. He'd been pushed along, that's all. By the poor example of his father, then by the army, and finally by Louise.

Well, he was exaggerating. But, damn it, he hurt. Inside, where ice was forming at the door of his heart, the rag-and-bone shop of his heart, the heart that he had opened to her, to Emily Parsons.

He loved her. It nearly stopped his breath how much. And how could that be? He was seventy-seven years old, not some hormone-driven adolescent. He could not have fallen so deeply in love in a matter of weeks. It wasn't reasonable. It wasn't something a rational human being did. Perhaps it wasn't real. Perhaps it had to do with something gone wrong in the aging brain, a misfire. Maybe he was simply afraid. Thom Koetters had married late, married a preacher's widow when they were both past eighty. But that had been for comfort, the cushions already broken in. It wasn't at all like this, what he felt. He couldn't find words for this. This was grander and more terrible than anything he'd ever known.

His boots crunched through dry leaves. His face had stiffened with the cold. *A man could die out here*, he thought. It was as good a way as any to go, better than most, or so he'd heard. You just went to sleep. There was something seductive in this cusp of winter, and it seemed to him that he had surrendered unknowingly, bit by bit, each of his senses. He heard and smelled nothing. His hands, pushed into the depths of his pockets, were numb. His toes disappeared.

He let his mind play with the idea of just plunking down somewhere, just like that, giving it all up. It was a reverie not unlike those he'd had as a child when, after suffering some slight, he'd pictured himself laid out in a pine box, somehow enjoying (though he was surely dead) the lamentations going on around him. The idea of his mourned-for self comforted him, especially in the night when he was most lonely and didn't know why.

Should he hurry his steps or slow them? Should he ease the mind of a woman who was surely worrying, a woman he claimed to love, or pay her back by dying first? "Serve her right!" he barked with a cloud of breath like a geyser into the air. He imagined her rising from the bed, calling for him. Confusion first, then alarm. "Serve you right, old girl. Do you hear that?" He punched the air for emphasis. The world came back, whiter and quieter. His legs ached from the cold and the exertion, and for the first time he began to entertain the idea that the decision whether or not to die in the snow might not be his.

What was getting to her anyway? Cancer, he guessed. Pancreas. Stomach. Something right there in the middle of things. It would be a bad end. He couldn't stand the thought of that, of her having to endure that. His mother had screamed hour upon hour in the end. Hers had been in the brain and they'd had to tie her down to keep her from tearing at her own face. Jeronimo had been twelve. He'd lived through that time in the recesses of his closet, a pillow over his ears, but he'd never stopped hearing those screams, and the echo of them when they'd stopped. There was little in those days to ease that kind of agony. There wasn't much more now. They made you endure it. Unless you could find a doctor with his compassion still mercifully intact, you had to go it alone. Jeronimo did not want that kind of end for himself, and he did not want it for Emily. There was no dignity in it.

Something, more a feeling than a sound, made Jeronimo raise his head. In his path, still as the statues he'd sometimes seen on people's lawns, were three deer, a doe and two half-grown fawns. They were watching him, had been watching him as he bumbled blindly along his half-erased path, head in the clouds. He stopped, breath caught in his chest, so close to them he could see the fine white hairs inside the fawns' ears. *Nothing living could be that still,* he thought, but it was a stillness on the edge of trembling. In the blink of an eye, at some signal he could not see, the two fawns leapt off into the trees, their mother a heartbeat behind. He watched their silent, graceful bounding until the snow reclaimed them as if they had never been there.

He began to hurry along now. He wanted to be with Emily, damn the consequences. He wanted to tell her about the deer. He wanted to share with her things about himself that he himself hardly knew. He wanted to be gathered into the warmth of her while he could. He wanted to hold her as she died.

He began to recognize landmarks as he neared the campground, a line of broken split rail fence, a solitary redwood with a lightning-blasted trunk. And then there it was, the old red pickup with its familiar dents and primer spots, the ladder still stretched its length and cinched with bungee cords. In his relief and joy he stumbled across the campground toward it.

"Emily!" he cried, as if to recall her from the dead had she, God help him, somehow slipped off while he was gone. He threw open the door.

"Mo!" she cried. "Where have you been all this time?" She brushed the snow from his shoulders and back as he clambered inside the camper. "Come and warm yourself."

14

The fire was just as he intended, huge, audacious. Flames licked and snapped at the black sky in which a sliver of moon lay like an empty porcelain saucer. Fanned out from where they sat hip to hip on the trunk of a fallen tree were the footprints he'd made in search of the wood to build the fire. It had not been easy to find kindling and broken branches dry enough to burn, but Jeronimo was determined that this fire, their last, would be his best. A statement, a final testament.

He could hardly see Emily's face for all her bundled clothing. Tucked in beside him, wearing his knit cap and checkered jacket, she looked like a small boy swamped in his father's clothes. She'd brought the army blanket from the camper, and that was wrapped around her too, but it wouldn't do much good after a while, not in the dead of night when the temperature plummeted. He'd have some talking to do to keep her out here. But for now she was warm.

She yawned twice. He wrapped his arms around her—he could have wrapped them twice—and he heard her start to hum. Some tune he didn't recognize. A waltz, or maybe a lullaby. How utterly lacking in self-pity she was. He didn't understand it. Given a death sentence, he'd have been howling on street corners, collaring priests and doctors, perfect strangers, bewailing his fate to the gods for whom he'd previously had no use.

Or would he? He didn't know. Nobody knew unless it was happening to them, and for a few minutes, though she was berthed safely within his arms, Emily seemed as far away as one human could be from another, as far as her stars were scattered each from the other. This is why he hadn't let her speak the words that took her already to that other place, why he'd put her off so long. Because he could not go there, not even in his imagination. He could not imagine now. In the place of imagination was only a dull kind of fear, nothing grand or exalting at all. Perhaps he was not as imaginative as he'd supposed.

He stared out into the dark, past the snapping, roaring fire, and told himself there was nothing to be afraid of. All his life he'd believed only evil of the things he couldn't see or didn't know. Death had been the worst of them, a faceless, patient stalker, the final terrible secret, the zippered black bag. Now, when the fire was gone and he and his Emily had dropped into sleep, death would be their friend.

He had broken down when she'd finally said the words, and

so had she, he on one side of the table, she on the other, their hands clutched across the worn Formica tabletop like shipwreck survivors across the upended prow of a boat. He would not release her hands even to wipe the tears. Never before in his life had he cried without a sense of shame for, as the Brits would have it, "letting down the side." But with her he'd begun to cross without even knowing all the lines he'd drawn for himself about what a man should and should not be.

It was she finally who sat back, wiping her eyes, even smiling a little. He read what she was thinking in her eyes. Would he smile? Never. He would never smile again, never laugh out loud to let in the light. All that was finished. In the lines and creases of her face—he knew them, every one—the tears pooled. For the first time since meeting Emily Parsons, Jeronimo longed to see her as the young woman she once was, just for a moment, just a glimpse. For the first time he felt cheated of all he might have had. She blew her nose, a good strong honk. Then she leaned forward again, covered his big hands with her own, and said with such urgency it frightened him, "Let's make this our good-bye, Mo. This moment. Right now."

He said he didn't understand. He was still sunk in his misery and he wanted to mire himself in it. He couldn't understand how she could be talking in normal tones, her face rekindled with life. Couldn't she see that he was dying too? And he began to feel resentful, as if she'd left him struggling alone in his sea of misery and swum to shore.

"How can I explain this to you, my darling?" she said. "This . . .

experience. This thing that I'm going through is new, brand-new. Horrible. Frightening. But . . . oh, I don't know what word to give it." She frowned, thinking. "Nothing fits. Challenging, I suppose, though that isn't right either. I'm feeling my way through, one step at a time, don't you see? Trying to keep my eyes open. Trying not to do this any other way than my own way. Can you understand?"

He nodded dumbly. He wanted to ask if she'd ever done anything in her life in any other way but her own. He doubted it. He knew that his better self should try harder to help her in this thing, but he hurt too much. He had let her into that deep and foolish part of himself that lived in terms of forever, and he'd been cheated. There was no forever, not now. He no longer even wanted one.

"I've even thought this might be a gift of sorts." She folded a tissue in half, in half again, and blew her nose. She looked up, again with that smile. "Not all gifts are those one would choose, are they?"

What was she talking about? This stuff about gifts again. What did that have to do with anything? If he weren't being his better self, he'd get her back on track. We're talking about the big D, Emily, he'd say. He was ready to take it on with her, lock horns with it right to the end, but you had to know the enemy. Couldn't namby-pamby around about it.

"I didn't tell you this before, Mo, but right after I'd been given the prognosis and I expected—oh, I don't know what I expected. To faint dead away, I suppose. The oncologist wanted to call Alison, have her come and collect me, but I wouldn't let him. I left the office under my own power. Walked outside into what had been an ordinary day—so odd, isn't it, one minute to the next and one never knows.

"I crossed the street to that little park, you know the one. With the lovely little Japanese bridge and all the native plants and winding paths. And it was extraordinary. I felt like I was walking above the ground, as if I'd already crossed over, into some, I don't know, some parallel universe. Isn't it odd? Everything glimmered with a kind of clarity and light I'd never experienced before."

She'd brought her thin spotted hands together at the point of her chin, and though she was gazing at his face, her gray eyes were far away. "And then something else happened." Her hands dropped away from her face and she sighed. "I began to think. I began to think that it, what I was feeling, was perfectly normal, given the circumstances. A protective sort of thing. Something with a Latin name, written up in all the medical books. And it went away. Just like that. Like it had never been."

"Shock," he said dully. "You were in shock. The mind has ways to—"

"Mo, don't you see? Don't give it a name. If anything, call it a gift. But I gave it right back. Because I couldn't understand how anyone in her right mind could be experiencing a kind of *ecstasy* at such an awful time, I talked it away. Analyzed it right out of being. And it was a gift, Mo, pure and simple."

He sighed. He frowned and fidgeted with his hands. Finally he stood and got their cognac glasses and the Courvoisier out of the cupboard. She watched him pour an inch for her and three for himself, what had become a nightly ritual. "And so is this," she continued. "This knowing ahead of time."

"How can you say that?" Agitated, he took the liquor in a single swallow, letting it burn away the ache in his throat. "I won't be able to think of anything else. I'll wake up every morning and look to see if you're still breathing. Better still, I'll go without sleep. That way I'll know when the moment comes. I'll see it, or feel it. Gift? Some gift. It's like getting a letter bomb in the mail. How can we pretend it's not happening, Emily? Use your head."

"Well, I think I am, Mo," she said quietly, reasonably. "I never said to pretend it's not happening. In fact, just the opposite. Knowing that it is happening changes everything. And it should."

How could she be dying when her eyes were so full of life? Perhaps it was a mistake. You couldn't trust doctors. How reliable was this doctor, anyway? Probably didn't even use the latest machines, the computer scans. Jeronimo tried to follow what Emily was saying, but it was hard.

His mind had been busy making its own agenda.

"How many hours of life have we been granted so far, Mo? Far more than most people on this earth. And how many have we simply passed through? Like sleepwalkers. We can't do that anymore, my darling. These moments—the ones that just passed, this one, this very one—are too precious, don't you see? We can't look at life the way we used to. Not now."

His soul felt sluggish, unresponsive. He sensed that she was right, but it took a kind of work he wasn't ready for, an emotional discipline he didn't have. It was easier to wallow, to surrender to the inevitable, to make peace with it. And, besides, he'd have to go it alone once she was gone. The very thing he'd tried to avoid by taking up with her in the first place. She didn't know what she was asking. There were better ways to do this thing. You didn't have to accept its terms, put a good face on it. You could choose when to bow out. You could do it with dignity. He would see to it.

Over her mild protest, he'd poured her another inch of cognac and filled his own glass. That was when she began to talk of going home, back to Santa Barbara. He let her talk. Already he'd made up his mind (and hers, how could he not?). He'd been almost light-hearted, agreeing to the hot chocolate she offered to pour into a thermos, lacing it liberally with cognac, saying that, yes, they ought to bundle up, but the fire would keep them warm as toast. And now she was humming and he had his arms around her. His fire sang and spat. Before she closed her eyes in final sleep, it would be the last thing she would see, this fire he had made for her. He was almost sorry not to be able to share this last thought.

"Mo?"

"Mmmm?"

"It's all right to leave, isn't it?"

She'd caught him by surprise, but then he realized she was back to talking about her family, that other leaving, about cutting their trip short. She'd been concerned for him. Imagine! She didn't want to ruin the trip for him. "Yes! Yes, it's the right thing to do," he said. "I wouldn't have it any other way."

He was almost gleeful. Like a small boy playing a trick. Then guilt crept up from behind and tried to bag him. He fended it off.

Someone had to think, to look ahead. Soon she would sleep and then, only then, would he let himself bound after her into the deep, snowy woods. They'd be found eventually, and someone would say he'd been a fool. He'd be blamed, of course, being a man. But he knew what he was doing all right. He had taken into himself the spirit of the bison.

"I don't know when it was," she said, "that I realized . . . oh! yes, yes I do. I'd gone out for water. For the coffee. When you were gone. Isn't it strange how the deepest truths can come at the most ordinary times?" She turned her face to his, and he saw all over again what he'd fallen straight in love with. What a ninny he'd been not to acknowledge that love straightaway. Time was all they'd ever had, and he'd squandered it right from the first.

He said he supposed truth could come like that.

"And that the deepest truths are so often, well, ordinary themselves."

Her voice trailed off, and she said nothing more for a while. Then she said her daughter's name. It came with a sigh. "The children are young," she said, carrying on some private argument he had only the thread of. "They have the protective callousness of youth. Still, they should have their chance to say good-bye. They're wonderful, gutsy children, you know."

He didn't care a fig about her grandchildren. They had whole lives to live. He didn't care about her daughter either. He hoped they'd feel the flaming pangs of hell when they learned of Emily's death. They deserved it, each of them. They'd used her, and they'd nearly used her up.

Well, what did he know really? He had read between the lines of the life she'd shared with him, that's all. She hadn't complained. But he sensed that she hadn't been happy. Some of her happiest days, she'd said more than once, had been in these past few weeks with him.

". . . it's Alison I'm concerned about. I take her so for granted, you see."

"The other way around, if you ask me." She hadn't, but what did that matter? This wasn't truth. It was a sentimental fiction of the worst kind. Didn't she see that?

"Every little line in her organizer book is filled. Imagine that. And I let that impress me. She's a desperately unhappy woman, Mo. She runs a corporation, not a family. No one ever talks or laughs or sings. They whine and gripe. The kids are frantic with misdirected needs. Alison is exhausted, worn out before the day begins. She no longer knows what's really important in life. And she was such a sunny child. I don't know what happened to change her, but she's lost."

He wished she wouldn't talk about her family. That was the other life. That was all behind them now. Todd wasn't lost. With Jeronimo's life insurance, he'd be better off than he was now. He was a grown person. So was Alison. Emily was behaving as if parenthood were a lifetime proposition. What could be more ridiculous? He'd been without parents from the age of twelve, for heaven's sake. What was she thinking?

And, yet, almost as if he'd come up behind them, Todd was here for him now. His mind tried to blink his son away but couldn't. He remembered too clearly watching Todd wedge the last box of books into the overstuffed van, wearing what Jeronimo came to think of as Todd's uniform—blue jeans, denim shirt faded almost to white. He had Jeronimo's height, Jeronimo's build, and yet he was not in any way his father.

You had to let go of your children or they would break your heart. Couldn't she see the necessity of that?

"She's still a child in some ways, Mo. Still trying to prove herself and running herself ragged in the process. She loves the children, but she hardly sees them, you know? She's missing out on all the beauty and meaning of a life."

"Well, you can't change her now." He wanted her to talk about the two of them, about him, about how much he meant to her. That was what he wanted to hear.

"Well, you see, that's what I realized going out for the water. If I rob her of this last opportunity, she may never turn that corner."

"What opportunity?" Would she never give it up?

"To help me die," she said. "It's my final gift, you see. And hers to me."

He shut his ears, his senses. He would not feel sorry in these last moments. He would not think of Emily's family, the spunky grandchildren. He would not think about Todd. He'd made the decision for both Emily and himself. She would thank him if she were in her right mind. And if there were an afterlife, she'd thank him then. He was certain of it, or certain enough.

"Let's go inside, Mo," she said. "I'm sleepy. How about you?"

"No," he said too emphatically. She turned her face to him, and he could see that he'd startled her. "Why go in now, when the fire's just gotten started? Here," he said, "snuggle closer. That's my girl. Now what do you see in the flames?"

"Nothing," she said sleepily. "My eyes are shut."

"Cozy, isn't it? Now you're warm, aren't you? This is an adventure. Staying out past our bedtime. Challenging the elements."

"Mmmm," she said and yawned. "My toes are cold."

"Put them closer to the fire." He reached down and nudged her boots closer to the flames, struck for a moment by the enormity of his own selfishness. In the next life, if there was one, he would come back as a saint, a martyr. He'd not have a single selfish wish. It was the law of averages, wasn't it? He would gladly make up for everything in the next life, if he could just have a little more of this life now. With her.

15

He was on the city bus. In his arms was a squalling infant wrapped in a gym towel. But it wasn't his, how could it be his? He and the professor were too old for babies, anybody could see that. They'd been having a delightful literary conversation when someone he hardly saw—dark and, he thought, hooded—dropped the child on his lap and scurried down the aisle to the exit. He turned to the professor, only to find that the professor was now a middle-aged woman dressed in a red kimono and reading the *Wall Street Journal*. Jeronimo knew without asking that the child wasn't hers. She didn't even seem to recognize his existence, much less the child's. Nor did anybody else. No one would look directly at him or at the boy—it could only be a boy—yet he knew they were sneaking glances because he caught several of them in the act, their faces twisted in a kind of fascinated horror before they quickly looked away. He jiggled the baby, patted its damp back. Something told him not to look too closely at this child. Something was dreadfully wrong with it. This was the reason for its anguished cries and also the reason no one would claim it. In exasperation, he turned at last to the woman beside him and said, "What do I do with this baby?" The woman glanced from the NASDAQ to the child, then to Jeronimo. Her face never changed its expression of bland, almost bored distaste. "Everybody's got it," she said. "What did you expect?"

He blinked open his eyes. The bunk. Morning. A snow-bright Montana morning. His glad old heart kicked up its heels. And then, like a knife to that heart, he remembered the fire, his dark plan.

He sat up, alarmed, confused, the sheet beside him rumpled. Where was Emily? He must have dozed off at the fire. How could he have done that? Where was she? Out there? Still out there?

"Emily? Em!" He threw his legs over the side of the bunk and felt his back wrench. His naked flanks shook as he descended the ladder. If she was out there, still out there by the fire . . .

He stopped short, one foot on the cold floor. But she'd led him in here, hadn't she? Or was that, too, a dream?

He climbed awkwardly into his blue jeans, his back refusing to bend. He welcomed the pain, crouched into it like a wounded animal. He was an idiot. He should be shot.

"Em!"

The door opened and she stuck her bright face through. "I'm right here. Why are you yelling?"

"I hurt my back," he cried, because he couldn't think how to answer otherwise. Giddy relief nearly swiped the legs from under him, and he grabbed the ladder for support. He hadn't killed her. "What are you doing with that coffeepot?"

"The pipes are all frozen, Jeronimo. I thought I told you that. So I've taken to gathering snow. It makes fine coffee, don't you think?"

Her eyes were alive this morning. The cold air lent color to her cheeks and she looked years younger. She looked as if nothing could take her down. For a moment he allowed himself to believe that.

"I'll rub you down with wintergreen," she said, climbing up, setting the pot on the counter.

"What?" Still caught between two worlds, the dead one and this. Or had they crossed over to the other side after all? How could you know?

"For your back," she said. She shrugged out of his checkered jacket. "We stayed too long out there in the cold. I could hardly wake you to get you into bed. You've stiffened up, that's all."

He tried to read her eyes. Had she guessed? He didn't think she had. She wouldn't be speaking so civilly to him had she guessed he'd been making decisions for her again.

Well, he had. Or tried to. The final decision. And he'd botched it. He watched her search the cabinet for the wintergreen, her brow furrowed with concern for him. But the pain had evaporated. His blood exulted. She was alive.

"When was the last time I told you that I loved you, Emily Parsons?" he said to her back. She was wearing the blue jeans she'd had on that day in the library and a bright red turtleneck sweater. Red gave her pale face color, borrowed life. She wore it often now.

She turned, amused. "Why, that's the first time, Jeronimo Smith. That's the first and only time."

"Not true," he cried. "Why, I must have said it a dozen times. At least a dozen times. You're slipping, Emily."

"Well, perhaps I am, Mo." She cocked an eyebrow. "And how many times have I told you?"

"Oh, all the time," he sang. "You tell me all the time. And I don't think you should stop, either. I don't think you should ever stop." His spirits, having hit bottom, were soaring now in delirious relief. And then he began to weep.

She held his face between her cool hands. He couldn't look away.

"I'm just going first," she said softly. "Someone has to."

"Why do you believe in it?" his worst self spouted. "Choose to believe what you want, you said. Why don't you choose to be well?"

His arms dropped and he let her go. He couldn't fight the thing growing inside her. He could only fight the woman.

She turned away. She looked out the tiny window at the blackened circle of their fire. "Don't you think I've tried?" she said. She turned back to him with anguished eyes. "Do you think I want this?"

"Then take me with you," he said.

"What?"

"We'll go together." He drew her down to sit beside him on the single bed. "Don't you see? That's what this adventure was all about. I didn't know it that night in your room when I asked you to come with me. How could I know? But now . . . *now*, it all makes perfect sense. We'll go together."

"Together? Surely you don't mean—"

"Why not?" he cried. "Why not? You're so all-fired stubborn about making your own decisions. Well, what about me? What about my decisions? It's my own personal decision to live or die, isn't it?

"But—"

"Well, isn't it? Isn't it? You can't change the rules to suit yourself, Emily Parsons. I don't *choose* to go on without you." The energy went out of him and his voice grew quiet. "I don't *choose* to believe that life can be worth living without you in it."

"Mo, you can't mean that." She looked at him as if he'd badly disappointed her.

"I do, damn it."

She studied him. She sighed through her nose. He noticed that her hands were no longer enclosed in his. "Arsenic?"

"What?"

"A bullet to the brain? What exactly did you have in mind? A drop over Angel Falls?" The gray eyes cool, steady, uncompromising.

He shrugged. He looked away. "Something . . . painless," he muttered. "Pills, maybe. I don't know. You don't have to worry about it. I'll think of something."

"There you go again," she sighed.

"Okay, then you do it. You decide."

"I'll decide no such thing, Jeronimo Smith. You're not going anywhere. At least not now. Not until your time comes. This is nonsense, all this . . ." Her hands fluttered in the air for words. "Nonsense."

His eyebrows went up. "Someone wants to die in your arms and you call it nonsense?"

"Bull crap."

His lips twitched, but he refused the smile she was courting. It had seemed so right just hours before, wrapped in the arms of the woman he loved, staring death in the teeth. Now he felt deflated. Useless.

"And, besides, there's Todd."

"Todd." There he was again, wholly materialized at the mere mention of his name. A name that a father argued at his son's birth—and rightly—was a sissy name. "Todd doesn't need me. I don't approve of the way he lives and he knows it. I can't change that. I can't change him."

She considered for a minute what he'd said. "It's crazy when you think about it, isn't it? The way we keep trying to change people. We all do it, and it rarely works. Particularly if they don't want changing. People were born to be pretty much who they are, who they were meant to be. And if they're our people and we love them, we let them be."

"You don't understand, Em. Todd won't face facts. It's not just that he loves . . . men." Jeronimo winced. "He loves . . . God, I don't know . . . *indiscriminately.* He's a sucker for a pretty face. A pretty boy's face."

"Let him go, darling."

"But I thought you said—"

"Let him go first," she said. "Right here, right now. Let Todd be Todd. And you be you." She squeezed his hand lightly and got up to turn off the stove.

He leapt up, hovering over her as she poured the coffee with her steady hand. "But I can't keep my mouth shut. I can't pretend to approve of his lifestyle when I don't. I can't let him risk his life the way he does."

"No, of course you can't." She laced his coffee liberally with sugar. Turning, she set the cups on the table and looked up. "Tell him the truth about the way you feel—I'm sure you do. But tell him all of it, Mo."

"All?"

"Tell him that you love him. That you need him. That you're desperately afraid of losing him."

Through the steam rising from his coffee cup the world beyond the tiny window looked watery and indistinct. His long life tunneled backward through pain and fear to its beginnings.

"Is that all it is—?"

"All?"

"The reason I blow it so often. Why I can't seem to control myself?"

"Could be," she said.

"Well, it can't be as easy as that, can it? That I've just been afraid? Bluffing?"

"Oh, you can control yourself, my darling. I don't believe for a minute that you're not your own person. But you feel things, Mo.

Deeply. And it scares you. You fend people off with your silly tantrums, mark up the world with your blue felt-tip pen. Better to be thought crazy than someone with real feelings. Men don't feel, they act. Another of those awful clichés that proves itself true."

"In the library that day—"

"Yes?"

"Did you know that? About all this *feeling*?"

"Nope," she said with a grin. "I thought you were crazy."

"I couldn't stop thinking about you," he said.

"Nor I, you."

He could no longer imagine living anywhere other than here, in this tiny cave where he knocked his knees and banged his elbows constantly, where he arose each morning knotted and cramped because the mattress was so thin, where you couldn't cook a decent meal or find a comfortable place to read. None of that mattered. As long as he had her. If only his plan had worked. He didn't know what to try next. A leap over the falls wasn't a half-bad idea, but she wasn't going to buy that.

"Together," he insisted, his hands holding the small, sharp bones of her shoulders. "Why not, Em? It makes perfect sense to me. It *does*."

"Mo." She shook her head sadly. "Darling." The tenderness in her eyes pained him. "You're caught up in your books again. Looking for the perfect ending. Ready to write it yourself, if need be." She reached up and cupped the side of his face. "Can't you just come as far as the gate? Holding my hand?"

His throat caught. "You don't know what's it like," he said.

"Of course I do. I've held some hands in my time. I know."

"The pain can be unbearable, Em. I've seen it. You'll wish we'd done it my way."

"Perhaps," she said. "We'll see. Maybe then . . ." She frowned. "But I don't want to hear any more about . . . about suicide pacts." She turned away from him and threw open the door. "Look," she cried. "Look what we're missing. It's glorious out here."

He stuck his head out and peered up at the mottled gray sky. "We could take that canoe ride you wanted," he said. "Let me check the weather." He stepped down and started for the cab.

"Oh, don't," she said. "Not now. I'm sure it's fine. Let's do take that ride. What fun!"

"Are you sure you're up for it?"

"It's a pretty good morning," she said, her hand on the place where the pain was stored. "And, besides, I've got my medication. A couple of these and you'd have to carry me home."

He raised an eyebrow. "You got enough for the two of us?"

"Enough!" she cried. "This is a day for living, not dying. What's the matter with you?"

16

The hiker came through the clearing onto a narrow strand of snowy beach, gravel and rock where the water lapped it clean. The lake's moonlight was ruffled up by an onshore breeze like a picture on a Christmas card, but the wind was icy and the hiker shivered in it, hands stuffed deep into the pockets of his down jacket. Christmas wasn't anything he wanted to think about. If he was lucky, he'd miss the occasion altogether, whiskey-soaked as a fruit cake in some Jackson Hole bar.

He'd been walking for days, stopping to rest briefly, eating nothing much, longing for something hot, hot coffee, then losing even that longing. Wilderness hiking could do that for you, wipe you clean of longing, of feeling. It was what he needed, or told himself he needed. His wife had left, this time for good. She'd meant it about the drinking. He didn't believe her then, but now he did, because she'd found somebody else. Lost in his own particular swarm of dark thoughts, the hiker followed the shore as it curved into a narrow cove.

He didn't know what it was at first when he came upon it, a carving of some kind, a Native American memorial, two figures in a canoe. Cast in silhouette against the full white moon, the couple looked too romantic to have been copied from life. The woman had a sweet rumpled face. The man's face was narrow and stern, with a long, hooked nose. Icy particles clung to the hairs in his nose.

Hairs!

The hiker cried out, a strangled, girlish scream into the dead-quiet stillness. They were real! *God!* They were real people.

Crying now between his curses, the hiker hauled the canoe up onto the beach, through screeching gravel, his breath streaming out with broken words, willing the pair to answer, to move. The woman's forehead lay in the scoop of the tall man's collarbone, his head rested at an impossible angle on hers.

He tried the old guy first. Freed the long, limp arm and felt for a pulse. Nothing. He tried the neck, and there, there! he thought was something, but his own fingers were numb and he couldn't be sure. "Don't be dead," he pleaded. "Goddamn it, don't be dead."

Beneath the black watchman's cap the woman's face looked peaceful, the way the dead were supposed to look and sometimes did. She looked as if she'd been dreaming of being alive. Her lips were purple, the color of ripe plums. She had no pulse either, at least none that the hiker could find in the thin, pale wrist. He slid her by the armpits out of the bald guy's embrace and hoisted her up into his arms. Then, as if the old guy had been supported all along by the frail woman and not the other way around, he pitched forward in slow motion and toppled into the pit of the canoe. The hiker began running toward the car with the woman, her small, booted feet bouncing lightly against his hip. Otherwise still, a still dead weight in his arms.

Or maybe not dead, please God not dead. Dead weight was heavier than this. He knew that.

Jogging back through the clearing, into the snow-clogged parking lot, he laid the woman like a bagged deer on the hood of an old red camper truck that was parked there. Her legs fell apart and he pushed them back together. He patted her hand, which lay curled on the hood like a claw. He pulled off his down jacket and laid it over her chest, tucking it around her. The cold came down upon him in a solid block.

The camper door was locked. The keys had to be, *had to be*, in the old man's pocket. The hiker's eyes searched the parking lot, the surrounding woods. He needed something to haul the old man with. A board to lay him on, a door. The one on the restroom was made to withstand full-scale invasion. He remembered medivac stretchers. He imagined the kind of contraption he might make with tree branches and rope, but there was no time.

Only then did he notice the ladder, or the ladder notice him, or so it seemed to his disordered mind. The hiker released the cords from the aluminum extension ladder and slid it from the top of the camper. He stuck his head through the ladder and settled it on his shoulders. His bum knee ached, but he knew how far he could push it. He'd been running for twenty years, why stop now?

17

The universe was thumbing its nose at Alison. Her mother lay dying in the upstairs bedroom, and there was nothing Alison could do about it. Frustration had fueled all her actions until now, but frustration had its limitations. Fuming, bellowing, threatening lawsuits, she'd gotten her mother home from the hospital in Jackson Hole in record time. She'd demanded that Emily's doctor be on hand when the plane landed at 3 AM. Over protests by the doctor in charge at Cottage Hospital, she had commandeered an ambulance to bring her mother home, only to learn from Emily herself that she'd been dying all along.

Frustration was nothing more than a thin blanket thrown over Alison's fears, but at least it had gotten them home and away from that fool—that crazy bald man her mother had run off with.

Alison didn't know what came after frustration in the chain of things, but for her it was nothing. Space. Space in which her body moved around and she got things done. Space in which the tentacles of her mind sent out exploratory feelers. Her mother had been here for such a short time, and yet Alison had come to count on her for everything, even for advice about her business dealings, which made no sense at all.

Well, it had nothing to do with real estate, her dependence on Emily. How could it?

What would happen now? Alison went into the kitchen realizing that what would happen was already happening. The children came in and out of her consciousness and she dealt with them: TC with his serial demands — in his bid to win the city's skateboard championship he seemed not to realize he was about to lose a grandmother — and Sam, her ever present roller-coaster moods now in full tilt. In her eight-year-old daughter, Alison recognized a mirrored image of herself in miniature. One minute Sam was her reasonable self, a model child, and Alison could count on her to do any one of the dozens of things that needed to be done for a bedridden grandmother on the second floor. But it was never long before she would spin out of control. When would her Nana get better? She needed her Nana to be well, to get out of that bed. Who would make the banana pancakes? For Sam these were the essential questions of existence.

And Emily herself, insisting on her upstairs bedroom when a bed in the living room downstairs would make her care that much easier. There were times when everybody seemed at cross-purposes, Alison as well. But instead of insisting that things be done her way, Alison seemed to be letting go.

Since bringing her mother home, she found herself doing the most uncharacteristic things. This afternoon it had all started with hot chocolate. "A good hot cup of cocoa" was how her mother put it. Emily had always made it from scratch with squares of baker's chocolate, tons of sugar, and whole milk. And the vanilla, of course, drizzled in as the milk heated.

Alison's memories of her mother began in the kitchen. Yet Emily always said she regretted not having had more time while Alison was growing up to prepare a "decent" meal or keep a clean refrigerator or scrub the floor the "right way," the way her neighbor Libby did it, with a scrub brush and bucket after bucket of rinse water. And it was true. Emily was far more likely to be found in the backyard, her fingers dug into clumps of chrysanthemums, her mind so far removed that it took a good tug on her sleeve to bring her back.

Where did her mother go? Where had she gone, literally, in her long life? In fact, nowhere. Nowhere other than Niagara Falls for a four-day honeymoon. Nowhere but her backyard, where she gazed off into the distance. Nowhere until that nut, Jeronimo, spirited her away. A thought glanced off Alison's mind like a tossed stone: Was it possible that some withheld part of her mother had been looking all her life toward this thing that came along only at the end of it? Absurd. But there it was, one of those strange thoughts that Alison's mind took up these days with or without her consent.

She remembered seeing a bar of baker's chocolate somewhere,

however long ago. In with the spices or behind the cereal boxes. She began emptying the cupboards, box by box, can by can, until every inch of counter space, the table, and even the kitchen chairs were filled. Hands covered with flour, sticky with spilled honey, she stood back and marveled at what had accumulated behind those doors: canned tomatoes as old as Sam, flour and cereal crawling with mutating life-forms, a green-plastic whistle that recalled the avaricious depths to which two perfectly normal children were willing to descend over nothing at all, three opened boxes of cornstarch, a jar of Gerber's baby carrots with the pudding-faced baby on the front.

No chocolate. She filled the teakettle instead. The cup of "good hot cocoa" was for herself anyway, not for her mother. It was meant to buoy her through what they still called "lunch," bits of soda cracker and chicken noodle soup that dribbled down Emily's chin onto a makeshift bib. She was embarrassed for Emily, though Emily seemed not at all embarrassed for herself. Alison did not see how she could stand to witness day after day the shrinking of her mother's mind and body. Yet day after day that was exactly what she did.

Two houses she'd listed months before sold within three days of each other. She had never even shown them. It was like a gift. How could she have paid the rent otherwise? And yet none of it mattered.

When her mother came back from her jaunt ("Adventure, darling," Emily insisted in her more lucid moments) something changed, was changing still. It wasn't as if she could put a finger on it or explain it or even, most of the time, admit to it. A feeling more than anything else, though it seemed more tangible than that, a little like new skin.

She set the last unchipped teacup and saucer on Emily's bed tray. Tea could be properly drunk only from bone china, Emily insisted, but there was just the one teacup from the set Alison had gotten when she first married. She added a coffee mug to the tray and, for the first time in months, thought about calling Richard. He would want to know about Emily, or would say he wanted to know (despite the fact that he was busily ignoring a second family on the way to creating a third), would say he was furious he'd not been told, if it came to that. She probed the wound where her first marriage had been, expecting all the old unhealed anguish, but there was none. Instead, she saw like a character from a favorite old movie the Rich of earlier days, the man who had dazzled her from across a pepperoni pizza. For the first time it all made perfect sense: falling in love, bearing children, even the divorce. Like the early moves in a chess game, predictable and necessary.

She heard the door slam and Sam's backpack hitting the floor like a rock. Sam's eyes grew wide as she walked into the kitchen. "What are you doing?"

Alison turned to her younger child with what she thought might be an answer, but nothing came out of her. Instead, she reached down and carefully unclasped a Barbie barrette that had slipped its mooring. She gazed into her daughter's troubled green eyes. She let the slippery yellow strands of hair sift through her fingers while Sam fidgeted. "Nana's going to be soooooo mad," Sam warned from under eyebrows lowered like storm clouds. "Nana likes things to be neat."

"Remember this cup, Sam?" Alison said. She reached for the Peter Rabbit cup she'd discovered in the cobwebs of the cupboard above the oven. Then, to herself: "No, of course you don't."

"It was your cup. You got it as a gift from somebody—I can't remember who—but I put it away because you were too young for it. And then, well, it stayed put away." She sighed, turning the cup to study its old-fashioned sketch of the anthropomorphic rabbit and his mother. "And now you're too old."

"Oh, no, I'm not," Sam cried, grabbing the cup, cradling it with both hands to her chest. "I'm going to show it to Nana. Did Nana give it to me?"

"I don't think so," Alison said. "It was . . . I think—" But she couldn't remember. It was eons ago, and yet Sam was a baby just the other day. How could that be? Where had the time gone? What had she been doing all these years? If she blinked again the children would be gone, off to independent lives of their own and, like the cup in the cupboard, she would have missed it all.

"It *was* Nana." Sam's eyes grew wide, apprehensive, as if something dark had risen up and drifted between her mother and herself. "Nana gave it to me," she cried. "I'm going to show it to her."

Alison cupped Sam's narrow shoulders with her hands and held her in place. "Sam," she said quietly. "You know what's happening to Nana, don't you?"

"No!" Sam cried and her eyes welled up with tears. Her shoulders trembled under Alison's hands.

Alison knelt down so that their eyes met. "Nana can't stay with us forever, darling."

"Don't call me that," Sam cried, tears glazing her freckle-spattered face. She tore herself from Alison's grasp. "Nana calls me that."

"Sam—"

But by the time Alison got to her feet, Sam was scrambling up the stairs, taking her newly claimed treasure to her grandmother. Alison's hands seemed to float of their own will after her daughter, then dropped to her side.

The endearment had come unbidden, not one she'd ever used in any context. *Darling*. No wonder Sam had fled. Not only was her mother home and tearing the house apart, she was speaking like an entirely different person, a stranger. *Darling*. And yet to herself the word had felt more than natural—it had felt absolutely right.

Alison poured hot water into the bone china teapot Emily had brought from home. She searched through the mess on the kitchen table far more patiently than she would have thought possible for the soda crackers. She lifted the bed tray and headed for the stairs.

TC answered the knock on the door. A gawky old giant with hairy nostrils and a sweaty work shirt filled the door frame. "We don't want any," TC said. That was what his mother said and it usually made them go away, all the weird ones selling whatever they were selling, Bibles and junk.

"Is your grandmother here?"

TC pulled the door so that only his face poked out between it and the frame. The old guy looked nuts. Or scared. Weird. "We're not supposed to talk to strangers," he said.

"I'm not a stranger," Jeronimo said. "I'm your grandmother's—" He searched for the right word, but there was none. It occurred to Jeronimo for the first time—how could that be?—that he and Em should have married, while they had the chance. In Las Vegas in one of those roadside dollhouse chapels. All that seemed so long ago, like fiction, as if there couldn't possibly have been a time when he didn't know Emily. They were lovers, but he couldn't say that, not to this boy. He settled with a heavy heart for "friend."

"She's sick," TC said flatly.

"Will you give her this?" With a trembling hand Jeronimo unfolded the envelope he'd stuck into his back pocket. He knew that Emily's daughter, had she come to the door, wouldn't have given him the time of day, not after hanging up on him so many times. But he had to try. "She doesn't want to see you," she'd insisted the first time he'd called. "She knows what you were up to."

"What? What?" Jeronimo cried into the receiver sticky with sweat that had sprung from his palm. But he knew. Emily thought he'd tried to take their lives again, but he hadn't. He *hadn't*. It was the storm. He was going to check the weather station before they left for the lake, but she'd hustled them out. It wasn't his fault!

TC scanned the face of the plain white envelope with his grandmother's name scrawled on the front. Since his report on the Unabomber for social studies he suspected it might be a letter bomb. "No way," he said, but when a five-dollar bill appeared in the old man's other hand, he pulled it and the letter inside.

"Give it to your grandmother when she's alone," Jeronimo pleaded.

TC, horrified that the old man was going to break down and cry, suppressed an embarrassed giggle. He slammed the door shut without saying what he'd do with the letter one way or the other. He could throw it in the trash compactor. Tear it up in tiny pieces and toss it down the toilet. Turn it over to the FBI. It could be a bomb.

Jeronimo turned from the closed door. He went around to the side of the house, past his love's staunchly defended patch of grass, and looked up at the window from which they'd climbed that moonlit night. He could still hear her chuckling as she fit her small feet carefully into the rungs of the ladder while he held it steady from below. She had an uncharacteristically deep chuckle that delighted him even then. Beneath her window again, he was as close to her as he'd been in days, in days and nights, and he could hardly stand it. He reached down and found a pebble, sailed it in an arc at the glass. It plinked off. An angry face appeared. Up came the window. Down through the space between Jeronimo and his Emily came the angry hiss of the daughter's warning. "If you don't get out of this yard right this minute I'm going to call the police."

"Emily!" Jeronimo cried like a crazed goose in search of its lost mate. "It's me, Mo!"

The window came down. Emily was in there, or the daughter would have shrieked her warning for all to hear. He thought his Em must be awfully sick or she'd have come to the window herself. Angry or not, she'd have faced him herself.

Jeronimo left the yard more despondent than when he'd come.

The letter he'd given the boy was his only hope. But what if she was too sick to read it? Or her daughter found it first?

He climbed up into his truck, folded his arms over the steering wheel, and laid his head down. He'd put a gun to his temple if he had one. There was no point in living any longer. He'd been useless before he met Emily, a grouchy old fart taking up space. Now that she was cut off from him, he was less than useless. He was a carcass, a desiccated carcass still sucking the worn-out tit of Mother Earth. He should just off himself and be done with it.

18

Emily's dreams were all about loss. About loss for which she was always somehow at fault. A dream would whisk her off somewhere, usually far from where she should have been. She would be having a lovely time or just an ordinary time in one of those strangely disorienting dreamscapes, and she would suddenly realize — as in those dreams when one realizes one is missing one's underwear or, worse, is completely naked — that she had forgotten something. She would look around in the unfamiliar place and suddenly re-member. It was the children she had forgotten. She had lost the children. Her heart would constrict, squeezed in the death grip of a cold fist. Her mind would rebound wildly between the dream state and near-consciousness, her whole being ill with terror.

Sometimes the children were her own: Alison as a toddler or the dying Evan left behind in the grocery store cart or in some dark boarded-up room she couldn't remember being in. Sometimes the child was Sam, sometimes TC when he was an endearing bright-eyed two-year-old. Sometimes Alison's children were her own. But always it was too late. Even if she knew exactly where she'd left them, there was never time enough to return, to snatch them from the eternally open jaws of inevitable disaster.

Always she would know that for just one infinitesimal moment she had chosen herself over them; she had chosen freedom.

Or she would dream about a man. And this was, in its way, as unsettling as any of the other dreams. At least in her dreams about the children she knew what she had done. There was this or that very real child, a child that—until the mistake for which she would cheerfully exchange her life—she had cherished and protected. In the dream about the man she was never quite certain what she had done to lose him, or whether in fact he and she had ever met. All she knew was that in him she had at last found her soul mate, the deepest, most intimate love of her life. It was like lifting one's face to the rain after drought.

He was ghostly, incorporeal, a tall man with a stranger's face, or Frank's face, though she knew it could never be Frank. Much as she'd loved Frank—and she had—theirs had been a trusting, satisfying friendship. A friendship she'd been more than content with. In fact, more than many couples had. And she would have continued to consider herself a contented woman had the dream man, or the phantom-in-the-dream man not appeared. And when she couldn't find him, or even know that for certain she'd ever even met him, she was left with the feeling that her life, no matter how rightly or carefully or dutifully lived, was only a half-life, a shadow life.

The dreams were placid enough on the surface—again she would be doing something quite ordinary, perhaps ironing, when the realization occurred—but there was always the undercurrent of nightmare, of the ground slipping out from beneath the ironing board and casting her, unfulfilled, into black emptiness. She would awaken or half awaken in desperation, having grabbed at the very last moment a jagged edge of kitchen linoleum, her legs dangling in space. Her mouth would be open, ready to call the intimate stranger's name, but he had no name, or none that she could remember.

In her lucid, fully awake moments she hated the drugs and put them off as long as possible. But she needed them desperately. The nurse from hospice was her angel, a enormous black angel who, while waiting for the pills to take effect, would cradle Emily's head in her arms and croon. She promised something stronger for later. She called it a "cocktail," as if they were going to a very exclusive dinner party one of these days and wouldn't that be just the thing?

Emily tried explaining the man in the dreams to Alison and to the nurse, but she knew she made no sense.

Loss was a fact of life. If you were in your eighth decade on the earth you had to know that. So she slept, learning a little more as she drifted about letting go of living, about accepting the final loss, the ultimate loss of her self.

Sam was often at Emily's side when she awoke, propped against pillows beside her in the double bed. Sam would have her pile of storybooks, the well-worn books Emily knew nearly by heart. But now the roles were reversed, and Sam did the reading. What she couldn't read, she made up, ever the resourceful child and, it seemed, a child with a surprising cache of kindness. Sam's voice was monotonous and soothing. Emily would drift off in the middle of *Charlotte's Web* and wake up in *The Phantom Toll Booth*.

Then she awoke to something she didn't recognize as one of the old stories. Sam was holding up a single sheet of paper and reading slowly from it, struggling over unfamiliar words, sounding them out. As if called by something outside herself and told she must pay attention, Emily painfully pulled herself into consciousness. "What are you reading, darling?" she asked, reaching for a tissue with which to wipe the spittle from her chin. She leaked now from every orifice, a sea creature returning.

Sam shrugged. "A poem, I think," she said. "It has lines like a poem." She turned the page so that Emily could see it. The fussiest handwriting she'd ever seen. That's what Emily had said to herself as she watched Jeronimo fill out the registration form at the Las Vegas hotel, the one with the flying woman's shoe. Mo! How could her dreams have forgotten Mo when all her waking life was filled with him?

"Where did you get that, Sam?"

"TC got it from some man," Sam said. "His name was Yeets."

"Yeets?"

"Yup. It says so here on the top. 'When You Are Old' by William Butler Yeets."

"Yates," Emily amended. "Read it to me, Sam. Start from the beginning."

"But I can't read poems, Nana," Sam said.

"Of course you can, my darling. It's just the same as anything else. Rest at the commas, stop at the periods. Go on. You can do it."

"When you are old and gray and full of sleep," Sam began, forehead scrunched, her finger running beneath the hand-printed words. "And nodding by the fire, take down this book"—Emily brushed the hair away from her granddaughter's green eyes—"And slowly read, and dream of the soft look / Your eyes had once, and of their shadows deep."

"Isn't that lovely, Sam?" Emily said, her throat thick with tears. She could see Jeronimo bending over the stationery as he wrote, his glasses having slid to the base of his long nose. She could see the microscopic hairs on his earlobes, hear him breathe, catch his breath and sigh. How close he seemed.

"It's not finished," Sam admonished.

"Then finish reading it," Emily said. She closed her eyes and let the words sink in.

"How many loved your moments of glad grace / And loved your beauty with love false or true; / But one man loved the . . ." Sam hesitated. "Pil . . ."

"Pilgrim," said Emily.

"Like in Thanksgiving pilgrims?"

"Like that," Emily said. "Go on, darling."

"But one man loved the pilgrim soul in you / And loved the sorrows of your changing face."

Tears were coursing down Emily's cheeks, but Sam in her concentration did not notice them.

"And bending down beside the flowing bars . . ." Sam released an exasperated sigh and looked down at her grandmother. "I don't understand this, Nana. Nana, are you crying?"

"It's all right, Sam. Finish the poem. Finish reading the poem as best you can."

Frowning, Sam continued. "And bending down beside the flowing bars / Murmur, a little sadly, how love fled / And paced upon the mountains overhead / And hid his face amid a crowd of stars."

"That was lovely, Sam," Emily said in a faraway voice. "Thank you. Now could you take your books to your room and let Nana rest for just a little while?"

Sam gathered up her books. "I'll close the door," she said proprietarily, "so that nobody can bother you."

"That's my sweet girl," said Emily.

Had Mo been here with her? Had he come and gone in person and not just in her dreams? It was so difficult to sort dream from reality. Next time she would hold on to him if it took the last of her strength. Somehow in her muzzy, drug-filled mind she would find the words she needed to say good-bye to him, to let him go.

Words. She'd grown up believing in deeds, not words. And so had Jeronimo. What a man did, her father said—as if he were making it up on the spot—was who a man was. Emily had assumed, growing up, that the same held true for women. Then Evan died, then her parents, then Frank. Each time, death stunned with the same mind-numbing intensity, and she would wonder if she had ever, while Evan or Frank or her mother was alive, told them how very much they meant to her. Or if she'd simply assumed that the work of her hands would have said it for her. Evan was too young to understand, true, but it wasn't just for those she loved that the words were so necessary. They'd have been for herself as well. A completion, a healing.

So she'd come home from Yellowstone with a head full of words and begun to dispense them as best she could. She told Alison how special she was. How strong and capable and spirited she'd always been. She recalled Alison's birth, told her again how she was named, took her through some of her own cherished memories: the string of dime store pearls Alison had chosen herself, then presented in wide-eyed rapture to her mother; Alison's first ballet recital (she was a tree); the broken arm she'd refused to acknowledge until the end of the softball game (she'd pitched a no-hitter). Alison had been speechless, shy, delighted, and finally overcome. She'd laid her head on her mother's chest and sobbed, then, laughing, helped Emily out of her soaked nightgown. "I love you so much, Mama," she said and marveled at the ease with which the words flowed out of her.

Emily had done the same for TC, who wriggled and hung his head and tried to escape, yet stayed because he did love his Nana. She'd been a constant in a world he'd already decided at the age of twelve was random and unpredictable. He stayed until he was sure she was finished, then darted out of her room, relieved and moved in ways he tried very hard not to understand.

But Sam had hunkered down like a pig in mud. She loved compliments, and she'd never doubted for more than three seconds at a time that her Nana adored her.

Emily drifted off into a vast sea of words, from which she would choose like a hundred of the rarest gems those meant only for Jeronimo.

19

Time had become her enemy. Emily awoke several times during the night and found herself staring at the blue neon numbers of her bedside clock—1:35, 2:51, 3:20. What sense was there in that? What difference did it make anymore? She considered the way her life was spent now, the way in which it was parceled up. How vain had been her brave little plans for the way her life would end. How blind. Precious little was under her own control. She was bathed, fed, set on a pot to pee. In an ironic, embarrassing, sometimes humorous way, life had come full circle. Still, she had this left, this control over time. She reached over and tipped the clock on its face. Now time was whatever she needed it to be, and the night was her own.

She gazed out the dark squares of her casement window, remembering that other night, a magical night, and Jeronimo's bald head gleaming in the light of a full moon. She had gotten up and opened the window to a whole new life. Now the window, in spite of her wishes, was closed. Alison would keep her from catching cold when she was dying of cancer. The room was stuffy and still, too still. She wasn't ready for stillness. There would soon be enough of that.

She hoisted herself up so that she was resting on her elbows. In the glow of the night-light her dresser and desk rose up the wall in dark, blocked shadows. At the end of the bed her feet made two peaks in the snowy landscape of her bedcovers. Further up, her abdomen swelled like a melon. She was a sight. She didn't need a mirror to confirm it. What she'd become was registered in the surprised or sorrowful eyes of those who came to see her. It shouldn't matter how she looked, it shouldn't. And yet it did. She sighed at the tenacity of her vanity that would die only when she did.

She kept the Yeats poem tucked under her pillow. Sometimes she would slip it out and read it again, famished for Jeronimo's touch, his wit, even his bombastic temper. She told herself it was fitting to end this way, with literature, as it had all begun. It was as she'd wanted, what she'd asked of him: to go on without her. Why did she expect now that he would come to her? It was over. He'd sent her the poem to read in his absence, to remind her of all she'd meant to him. She respected that decision. Though her heart ached, she even admired it. He was moving on. As he should. Her soul cheered and died by turns.

She heard a siren a long way off, muffled by her closed window.

She pushed back the bedcovers and sat. One's goals, she reminded herself, were always relative. If she could cross the floor and open her window she would have accomplished a task as great as anything she'd ever done. It was worth the try in any case. She set her feet on the floor. The pain, dulled by the drugs or white-hot and searing, her ever present companion, accompanied her everywhere. With one hand on her swollen abdomen like a woman in the throes of labor, the other on her bed, Emily set out to conquer the territory of her room. Bathed in sweat, she crossed the floor one agonizing step at a time. At last she reached the window and laid her perspiring forehead against the cool glass.

He could have used a moon tonight, but he was probably luckier not to have one. Jeronimo cruised to a stop on Laguna a half block from 467, a house he'd have passed by just months before without giving it a second glance. To think of that. Cutting the engine, he slid across the seat and got out the passenger side, the door that didn't squeal. He pushed the door closed, stopping to listen for signs that he'd been detected, but the neighborhood was quiet, houses battened down and dark. He went to the back of the camper, opened the door and slid out the bulky canvas bag. He hoisted it up into his arms. Already his back protested. Half a block. His back would have to hold out.

As on that moonlit night months before when he'd hauled the ladder across the newly cut lawn and laid it against the side of Emily's house, he had no idea beyond the act of doing this one simple thing what would happen next. It didn't matter. If she didn't want to take him with her—she didn't—she'd have to see him at least, touch his hand just once more, look into his eyes, and he'd be saved.

Not that Emily was a saint. She'd have hated that. Still, that was the essence of the feeling he carried along with the canvas bag onto the buckled sidewalk of Laguna Street, the feeling that would cement spirit to action, at least for the time being. He'd left his house at ten past ten, unwilling, unable to wait a minute longer. It was a school night, he reasoned. The children would be asleep, or should be. He hoped Emily's daughter wasn't a night owl.

Buzzard was more like it. Turkey vulture.

The windows of the small two-story were dark, as he'd hoped they'd be. Jeronimo slipped through the sagging gate, went around to the side of the house and laid his bundle on the ground beneath Emily's window. He looked up, thinking he should have brought the ladder, wondering if he ought to go back for it. But it was enough for the moment that he was this close to her. He unrolled the canvas tent and the ground cloth. The stiff plastic crackled as he spread the tent carefully over it. He worked mostly by touch, lighting his penlight only when absolutely necessary. At one point something furry brushed his ankle and he yelped. His penlight found the cat, the same orange tabby that had watched him cut the lawn. When Jeronimo set the center pole and the tent rose, the cat marched inside. Jeronimo tried to retrieve the cat, but it was pitch-black inside and he couldn't see where the thing was. "Shoo!" he hissed, waving his arms blindly. "Shoo!" His arm knocked the center pole and the tent caved in on top of him, the cat falling on his chest with a soft, hairy thump.

A siren screamed. He jumped, his hand went straight to his heart, but the siren moved on, into somebody else's neighborhood, somebody else's life. He stood looking up at the dark squares of Emily's window, willing her to appear. When she did, or a vision of her did, he blinked in disbelief and she was gone. He moved instinctually, heedlessly, fearlessly, without his accumulated aches and pains, across the lawn, through the back door that someone, thank the gods, had forgotten to lock. He made his way through a crowded kitchen, found the stairs, bolted them in his bare feet three at a time. At the top he paused to orient himself, his breath ragged and quick. Hers would be the last door. He crept down the hall, his senses keen to the slightest sound. Stopping at Emily's door, he turned the knob quietly and pushed it open.

Emily lay in a small white heap beneath her window. Jeronimo moved across the room as if through water, through a dream, to her side. Kneeling, he gathered her into his arms.

20

Long into the night Jeronimo held Emily's curled back against his chest. If life left her, he would know it at once. It took all his concentration, this monitoring, so light and shallow was her breathing. Not so his own. He breathed her deeply into the empty places of himself, filled himself with her. To all the scents of her body that he'd borne in his olfactory memory was added a new smell, the fragile papery smell of dead leaves.

He'd begun drifting off when he heard her speak his name. His heart went wild. "I'm here, Em," he croaked.

"Where?"

"Right here," he said, pulling her closer, out of reach of all her dark fears.

"But where?" she insisted. "Where are we?"

He clicked his penlight on, found her face, her eyes. She was as alert as he was. "We're in my tent," he said gleefully. "I spirited you away again."

"But where?" she said, this time plaintively, her mind slipping. He watched her go, unable to hold her eyes in his own, to turn away the fear. And then she was gone. He held his ear against her lips. Sleeping. He closed his eyes, relieved, weary beyond feeling. He drifted off holding her in his arms.

Sometime later he felt her stirring. "Mo?" she said. "Where are the stars?"

He hesitated before answering. Did she think they were still in Yellowstone? And if so, why not let her? "They're still up there," he said.

"I can't see them," she said.

He considered for only a few seconds before digging through his knapsack for his pocketknife. Reaching up, he sawed three sides of a square in the heavy fabric. "There," he said triumphantly as a flap of canvas fell in. "There are your stars."

He lay back down beside her, slipped his arm under her head and drew her close. "So alive," she whispered, looking up at the strewn stars. "It's as if they're all talking at once, passing on what they know before it's too late, their little truths." She chuckled. "Big truths, I suppose they are, considering the size of the universe."

"Such a romantic," Jeronimo said, thrilled to be caught up in her game. "What if they're all, I don't know, *cussing?* Cussing each other out. All at the same time. Or whining about the size of the crowd. Gossiping behind one another's back."

"You don't believe that for a minute, do you?"

"I guess not," he admitted. "At least not when you're here."

"It's love that drives the universe, Jeronimo. And tolerance. Generosity. It has to be."

"And why is that?" he said, delighting in what he'd once have branded as the most sentimental hogwash. "Why does it have to be?"

"Because I said so."

"Ah."

"And because I choose to believe it."

"Yes."

"And because nothing else makes as much sense."

He almost asked her what sense had to do with it. Her dying made no sense. Not now. Not after such a short time of having her to himself. Dying in the abstract made sense. You couldn't people the world endlessly without somebody getting off the bus, everybody eventually. But her dying, that was something else.

"Jeronimo, have you called your son?"

He was ashamed to admit that he hadn't. "But I'm going up to find him," he said, surprised by the strength of his conviction. Todd could live wherever he wanted, he was a grown man after all, but if he needed Jeronimo, ever, for anything, well, his father would be there for him. If at all possible, with his big mouth shut.

"I left instructions for Alison," Emily said after a while. "Should have done it long before this, I know. Along with my will."

"Ah." His stomach clenched, his mind tried to lock down. He

didn't want to hear this, didn't want to think ahead, not five minutes ahead of these few minutes they had.

"I went back and forth for a couple of days," she sighed. "Coffin or urn, urn or coffin. Casket, I guess they call it now. As if it makes a difference. I couldn't decide. I guess I thought it should matter one way or the other, but I'm afraid it doesn't. Isn't that awful?"

"I don't think it's so awful," he said. "What difference does it make?" They were back in sync, as they were in all the important things. Why make a bigger fuss in the end than you did in life? Though in his case, it probably wasn't possible. He wished she hadn't brought the whole thing up. He didn't want to think about what would happen later when he'd lost her again, this time for good.

"I'm to be cremated," she said.

"Ah."

"It makes more sense environmentally, don't you think? And it's cheaper if you don't go for the extras. And besides," she chuckled softly, "I do believe I've had enough of the cold."

"Damn it, Emily, how can you joke at a time like this?"

He felt her laughter bubbling as if, even in her weakened state, she couldn't be contained. "Gonna get me a good hot fire going."

"Em!"

"Come on, Mo," she sighed. "Where's your sense of humor? Who says we have to put on our longest faces in the end?"

"You want a wake, is that it? You want us all to get drunk and dance on your casket?"

"Well, I don't want a lot of muling about, I can tell you that.

Friends come and visit now with their serious, sad faces, and I have to comfort them. Laugh with me, I want to say. Laugh with me while I'm still here."

"Easy for you to say," he muttered.

"Anyway, there won't be a casket to dance on, Mo. You can waltz with my urn if you'd like."

"With your ashes, you mean."

"I'll be light on my feet!"

"Stop!" he cried. "Enough!"

Later he was sorry. "Em?"

"Mmmm?"

"Are you all right? Are you in pain?"

"Yes," she said. "And yes."

"Shall I get your medication? I didn't think—"

"Mo?"

"Right here, Em."

"Do you have your blue marking pen?"

Marking pen? Her mind went off on tangents now. The drugs, he thought. He did his best to follow. "Somewhere," he said. "Why?"

After she told him, he chuckled to himself for a long time. What a treasure she was. She hadn't gone off on a tangent after all. She just wanted to have the last word. "I know they probably wouldn't bother with it," she said, "with dyeing my hair if I'm to be cremated. Still, you never know these days." He lay with her in his arms, forcing himself into wakefulness again and again, willing the night to last into another life, one they could enter together the way he always wanted it.

Near dawn she awoke in great pain and he hurried with her in his arms back into the house. Her face was contorted, her breathing labored. He laid her down on her bed and grabbed up one of the pill bottles from her bedside table. Holding it at arm's length, he squinted at the label. "Which one?" he asked, desperately grabbing a second bottle, then a third. Her head whipped back and forth on the pillow. She moaned through pinched lips, her face bathed in sweat. He chose a bottle at random. "For pain," he thought it said. He pried open the childproof lid with his teeth. Lifting her on his bent arm, he held one of the pills to her lips. "Can't," she gasped, turning her head away.

He stared at the bright orange pill in frustration. Surely she hadn't been swallowing these things. They were the size of bullets. He felt helpless. She gasped, her eyes dark with anguish. He didn't know what else to do. He popped the pill into his mouth. It was bitter as bile, but he chewed it. Then he put his lips to hers and, bird-like, fed her the medication. She struggled to swallow. He reached for the plastic cup with the bent straw. He held it to her lips, but she pushed it away. With his balled-up handkerchief he patted the perspiration from her face, cleaned away bits of orange pill that clung to her chin. Her eyes were fixed on his face with something he couldn't read. Her lips twitched as she tried to speak.

"Rest, Emily," he said, and she closed her eyes. "Rest, my love."

But just as he thought he'd gotten her settled, her eyes snapped open. "What?" she cried.

"Shhh, shhh," he said, smoothing her forehead with his big, useless hand. "Rest."

"What did you say?" Her eyes were wide, filled with fear. She clutched at his arm and tried to struggle up from her pillow. "What? I can't hear you!"

"I said to rest. Rest now, Em." He pushed gently against her as she struggled. "Shhh. Stop now. Rest." Horrified, he watched her shrink back, pushing against his hands as if she no longer knew him. "Em? Em, what is it?"

She twisted away and inched herself across the bed, where she crouched like a cornered animal. Her frightened eyes, wide, pupils dilated, no longer saw him. "They're coming," she cried.

"Shhh, shhh. It's all right, Em," he crooned senselessly, going to her in slow motion across the bed. He touched her cheek. He cupped her face in his hands. He saw himself coming back into her eyes and was for a moment relieved.

"Mo," she whimpered, clinging to his shirt. "They're coming, Mo. When I close my eyes I see them plain as day. So clearly, every face, and it's terrible. *Terrible.* I thought I'd know them, Mo. I thought you were supposed to know the ones that come for you, but I don't. I don't know a single one." She searched his eyes for answers he didn't have, then finished in a heartbroken sob: "They're all strangers. *Strangers.*"

Her words chilled him, but he held on to his reason, tried to feed it to her like he'd fed her the pill. "Em, listen to me. I'm right here. Nobody's here but us."

Her eyes darted past his face toward the open window. "No!" she cried. "No! Oh, Mo, you don't understand." Her strength gave out, and she dropped against his chest, whimpering softly.

He clutched both her hands, held them curled between his chest and hers, shook them a little to make her listen to him. "It's me, Em," he cried. "It's your Mo. No one's coming. No one's here but me. It's all right, Em. Open your eyes."

She raised her head. Tears streamed from beneath her closed eyelids into the cracks and crevices of her face, and he realized he'd been crying along with her. His nose dripped, and he thought what a pair they were. He wanted her to laugh with him, to ride above this thing as she'd asked all along. What a fine pair we are, he'd say, and she'd laugh and they'd blow their noses and go on, just as before.

"It's all right, my love," he crooned. He gathered her into the cradle of his arms, held her against his chest until the tension left her body and she slept.

He wondered what would happen in the morning when the daughter found them, but it didn't matter, not now, not this moment. Heavy and dull with the deepest weariness of his life, he held Emily against his thudding heart, too tired to think, to care about what would happen later. Finally he laid her down, smoothed her flannel nightgown, pulled the blankets to her chin. He brought the chair from across the room and slumped into it.

Several times he drifted off, his chin dropping to his chest. Each time he awoke he felt yanked against his will into a grim and sour consciousness. But then he would sense that she was still with him, that she hadn't yet gone, and his heart, ready to crack apart for the last time, would settle into its stubborn, plodding every-day rhythm. As the room began to lighten with the dawn, he stood and stretched, surrounded by the cabbage roses on her wall and memories too young to be memories. He crossed to the window and looked down at his sorry old tent with the hole in it. He would leave it for the boy. He would tell him to listen to his grandmother's stars.

Through sagging telephone wires and the shaggy tops of palm trees, he watched the sun wash the gray morning sky with brilliant bands of pink and pale orange. One part of him marveled, couldn't help it; the other part drew back, mulish. Without her, his mind insisted, without her there was nothing. He listened sullenly as a single bird, then another, heralded in the face of what he felt to be overwhelming odds, the continuance of life.

"Mo?"

He turned from the window, his heart lifting. She was sitting up in the bed, her face and nightgown bathed in the pinkish-golden glow of dawn. "Mo?"

"Yes?" He hurried over to her, ready to embrace all the miracles he'd never before believed in.

"Be very quiet," she whispered, her eyes wide and glowing, conspiratorial. "They've come. They're here now."

He perched carefully on the edge of her bed, caught up in the transfigured beauty of her face. With surprising strength she gripped his forearm with both her hands, and he held himself very still, barely breathing. "Who's here, my love?"

"The strangers," she said, as if he shouldn't have to ask. He turned to see where her eyes had gone. The window was filled with golden light. "Beautiful strangers."

"Strangers?"

"Yes! Yes!" she insisted. "See them? See?"

All he could see was the golden light reflected in her eyes. Then her hands lost their grip and she slumped softly into his arms. In his every cell he felt the life go out of her.

When Jeronimo knew for certain that Emily had left him he smoothed the surface of her pillow and laid her down. Then as the room filled with the clear, cruel light of morning he sat, her hand curled inside his.

This is it, his mind insisted, this is it. For so long, it seemed, he'd held the fear of this time, this moment, deep within himself, the moment of her death. Carried it like a live bomb, railed against it, argued with it, cringed in the corner of it like a confused and frightened child. And yet for some reason that he did not understand and perhaps never would, it was the most peaceful moment of his long life.

He'd memorized that face in the little time he'd had with her, or tried to. All its changes, its expressions. Her anger, her passion, her humor, her love. Her love. The fire in her gray eyes. The way they lit up when he came back to her after the shortest of absences.

This was a new face, smooth, translucent, a face from which worry and fear and even her love had been erased. He did not know how to read it. It locked him out, and for a time he felt himself pulling away, resentful because she had left him. His mind reminded him of his foolishness, that he had come to count on her too much, that he should never have loved with so much of his heart. She was not here to tell him how to feel, what to do, how to go on. It was a mistake to love so deeply. There was no way to come back from it whole, and now he was doomed.

Then something very strange happened. It was as if he'd gotten up and taken a step back from himself. Standing there — outside, as it were — he listened to the chatter going on in his head. It was odd, this being outside himself. He realized things he'd never thought about before. Putting up with all that chatter was like having a grouchy next-door neighbor, the kind who borrowed all your tools and never returned them, the kind who saw signs of rain in the clearest sky and dog crap on every sidewalk. The neighbor you put up with year after year because he wouldn't move away. What Jeronimo realized, standing outside himself, was that for the seven-plus decades of his life he'd been his own worst neighbor.

He'd been fixed in time for so damned long, thinking the same old things in the same worn-out ways, reading the same books over and over again, not to find new ideas he might have missed the first time around but to confirm what he already knew. His judgments were set in stone, his opinions the cement that held the stones in place. He had only to chip off what he considered fitting for any given situation, no matter how unfamiliar, no matter that the world had changed in a billion baffling ways since he'd entered it and that people had changed too. His mind and heart had petrified.

Somehow she had brought him through. Reached out her hand and pulled him shivering into the real world. For a while he clung to her vision of things. He thought: *If she can love me, I must be all right.* He'd had the good sense to trust her. His better self began hanging around for longer and longer periods. Several times he'd summoned up the courage to peek over the edge of his battered shield and found to his surprise that the field was clear. The enemy had decamped. People had changed. They were funnier, wiser, kinder than the ones that used to be out there. He didn't know how that could possibly be, but it was.

Sure, the world still had its jerks. What was the world without a few jerks? There were worse things, too, and always would be. People damaged beyond repair populating the earth in what seemed ever greater numbers. His heart flooded with sadness when he read about stolen children, battered wives, parents murdered in their beds. Some things went on in the same mind-numbing ways, and he supposed they always would. And he felt the same paralyzing frustration at his inability, at his country's seeming inability, to stop a tidal wave of violence. He wasn't a fool. Frustration was a sane response. He would continue to write his letters of protest to the *News Press*, correct mangled grammar wherever he found it with his blue pen. He would go on feeling sad and somewhat useless. But she had taught him to open his heart, that he could survive with his heart wide open. He could let people in, he could let the sadness in. He would not die of it.

"Mommy! Mommmmy!"

Alison swam through a damp web of sleep toward the insistent cawing of a crow. The great black bird tugged and tugged at her arm. She shook it off, but it wouldn't give up. Flopping over on her back, she opened her eyes. Sam. Sam in near-hysterics, pulling her into consciousness. "There's a man in Nana's bed!" she cried. "Come! Come and see."

Alison sat. Her head felt stuffed with cotton. "What man?" She'd had some terrible and unfamiliar dreams, anxious dreams in which she alone was responsible for solving everything from AIDS to world peace. At first Sam just seemed just another feature of her dreams.

Then she remembered.

She pushed the blankets back. She got up and threw on her robe. "Stay here," she said grimly. She lifted Sam and plunked her into the bed. "Stay right there."

When the door flew open and Alison appeared with her Medusa hair and wild eyes, Jeronimo held up his hand like a crossing guard and she froze in the doorway. "She's gone," he said quietly. He gave Emily's hand a final squeeze and stood.

Alison raised her hands helplessly, then braced herself within the doorway. Her mouth worked, but nothing came out. Just when he thought she might collapse, she gathered herself and leapt for him. Strangled by tears of grief and rage, she clutched his shirt collar in both fists. "You!" she wailed. "You took my mother."

He grabbed her hands and forced them still, forced her to look at him. Slowly he shook his head. At last she accepted the truth in his eyes and her hands dropped away. "We stole some time together, that's all," he said, but it was a sorry excuse and he knew it. He'd had Emily all to himself in the final moments of her life and he would do it all over again if he could. He would steal those last moments with brazen indifference for anyone else and suck the marrow from them. His better self could go to hell.

He turned away and walked to the window. Emily's daughter was not the monster he'd wanted to make her. How could she possibly understand—a woman so young, a woman whose life was all before her—what things came down to in the end? Like a child, she thought her life was already over, at this very moment, because her mother had been taken from her.

Jeronimo stood at the window gazing down at his tent, listening to Emily's daughter sob and keen. He knew he should leave. He'd had his time.

He turned from the window and saw to his amazement that a very small angel had entered the room. The angel's hair lay in pale blond strings on the wings of her shoulders and her face was splattered with freckles. She looked up at him, lips pursed. Then she said in a high-pitched, most disdainful voice: "You're a bad, bad man, Mr. Yeets."

21

Jeronimo went through the broken gate up to the front porch, where the door was ajar to let visitors enter at will. He could see several people already milling around inside as if at a birthday party. He thought about the old days, when black crepe was hung at the door as a matter of course. You knew what to do when you saw that. You knew the tenor of things. There would not be a party inside. You set your face for a solemn occasion. You thought dark thoughts. You went in to respect the dead, solemnly, and with a quaking heart. After all, it could be you.

These days you didn't know what the hell to expect. In the past three years he'd been to an Irish wake, a Buddhist flower ceremony, and a full Catholic Mass. No telling what would happen here. He only hoped Emily'd had something to do with it. He slipped into the house without anyone noticing him.

As he entered the living room, his eyes went straight to the urn. It was far better than he'd imagined it. Tasteful in its way. He'd expected less of Alison and was grateful. Surrounded by flowers, squat in the center of the coffee table, the urn looked like a burnished silver ostrich egg.

There were flowers everywhere, on every available surface, across the mantel, up the stairway. Each bouquet seemed to mock him. He hadn't been Emily's whole existence after all. Others, other people, were woven into the tapestry of her life. He stood behind an overstuffed armchair watching people enter. Their eyes were drawn immediately to the urn, as his had been, just as they would have been drawn to Emily had she been there in life. He looked down and saw that he had been standing on the sleeve of a bright red sweater. It had escaped from beneath the chair like a call for help. Jeronimo bent down and saw the dozen other things stuffed there. He picked out a round pearl button, thinking it might be one of Emily's, and slipped it into the pocket of his navy-blue suit.

Among all the people who had now gathered, Jeronimo recognized Emily's rabbi friend because he was the only person wearing a yarmulke. The rabbi had a starved and serious face, but his eyes bubbled over with what Jeronimo thought must be unrabbinical humor. Jeronimo was prepared to like the rabbi because Emily did, but he thought the humor out of place. How could anyone be smiling when the world had lost an Emily? But others were smiling, too, talking quietly in twos or threes. He heard her name several times, and he could see that they were remembering her as they should, as she was—a lovely, sensitive, caring woman—but he resented them all nevertheless. He wanted tears and pain and the gnashing of teeth. He wanted the ceiling to crack open. He wanted the earth to swell and grieve.

"No blue hair!" he heard from across the room. A short round fellow in a slate-gray suit and vest had thrown up his hands in a gesture of surprise. He'd been talking with Alison, whose brown hair had been gathered up and stuck to the back of her head like an oversized bagel. "No blue hair," he repeated, shaking his head slowly in disbelief. Jeronimo edged closer as the man's voice dropped a notch. "I rarely come to these events, as you can imagine," he said, leaning toward Alison. "I mean, I'd have to attend them all, wouldn't I? Unseemly for a funeral director, don't you see. But I just had to come to this one. What a gal she must have been. The nerve! The chutzpah!"

After a moment's confusion Alison, her mouth pinched, glared straight across the room at Jeronimo. He shrugged helplessly. Can't you see? he wanted to plead in Emily's defense and his own. Can't you see the fun she had? He hoped someday Alison would understand how a woman might want to dictate all the terms of her life, down to her very last words. Emily's daughter would have to live with the fact that someone had the gall to write NO BLUE HAIR across her mother's chest with his blue felt-tip marking pen.

From wherever he stood, Jeronimo's eyes returned and returned again to the silver egg that held Emily's ashes. He wondered where

Alison would keep it. In some cluttered closet gathering dust, he supposed, with the shoe polish and plastic grocery bags, waiting for someone to notice it and wonder how it had gotten there in the first place. He longed to gather up the urn and cradle it in his lap. He wanted to stand guard over Emily's ashes like a lion or haul her up like an eagle into the far reaches of a Wyoming sky. It was all too civilized for him, this Sunday-come-to-meeting affair, this gentle gathering of gentle friends.

"Shall we begin?" The rabbi had taken a spot between the couch and coffee table and stood with his hands crossed, waiting. The hum of conversation dropped off and he began: "You might be surprised at my being here and, I must admit, I am a little surprised myself." He smiled and went on. "But my good friend, Emily Wardlaw Parsons, called on the telephone not long ago, from Las Vegas of all places. She asked me if, in the event of her passing, I might say a few words to you, to her friends and"—he nodded toward Alison, who stood in a damp daze behind her solemn-faced children—"her dear family. As you know, Emily did not espouse the Hebrew faith, nor any, shall we say, 'traditional' faith while she lived, and yet she was among the most spiritual people I have ever known. I told her that, of course, I would be honored."

Wardlaw? What kind of a name was Wardlaw? And why hadn't Jeronimo heard it before this? How could a man share the intimate secrets of a woman's heart and mind and not know her full legal name? Her dead husband's name had been Frank, she'd told him that, but Frank Parsons had always been a distant, harmless ghost, a fictional character. Now Emily's Wardlaw life presented itself, and a far longer life it was—by years, decades—than the one she had had with him. He listened halfheartedly to the rabbi warming to his task. Some things the rabbi said Jeronimo concurred with, others struck his heart with all he didn't know about Emily and that other life. She read to the blind, spoke fluent Japanese (as if French weren't already enough). She'd graduated from Smith, he knew that, but summa cum laude! He knew she'd once written a garden column but not that she'd had a rose named for her. Jeronimo shot an accusing glance at the urn. Even if they'd had the time, he doubted she'd have told him half the things he didn't know. Humility. What good was it? If Emily were here, he'd give her a good piece of his mind.

He heard his name and came winging back to the rabbi's words. ". . . Jeronimo Martin Smith," the rabbi said, reading now from a text, "my Mo, who filled the last weeks of my long life with the extraordinary gift of his love." All eyes turned toward Jeronimo. He swallowed. He swallowed harder, but there was no holding the tears back. They leaked as if from a broken main and gushed out of his eyes. They rolled down his face and soaked the front of his white dress shirt. In this latest and, he was certain, last incarnation of his life he was a leaky old bladder—and it didn't matter a damn, not a damn.

People began speaking up now in response to the rabbi's request, sharing stories, eulogizing the woman he loved. He'd be expected to say something, he knew that. Something grand and fitting, the perfect thing. But there was never a breach into which he could leap. Someone was always there before him, saying the exact perfect thing each time. At last he jumped in on top of someone else: "She was my whole life!" he cried, his voice cracking. There was a brief, stunned silence. Then people began talking all at once.

Jeronimo stood in the middle of the room gazing distractedly at the tops of heads, at the white flakes scattered like salt through the funeral director's thinning dyed black hair. Jeronimo was a good six inches taller than the tallest person in the room (a woman), though that didn't, he knew, make him a bigger man. Some of Emily's friends smiled sad little smiles at him, some avoided his eyes. They didn't know he'd said the perfect thing.

He hung behind as others left the room. He knew that some would return, balance paper plates filled with food on their knees and talk of mundane things. Others would gather at the rented umbrella tables set up in the backyard—it was his mower that made it possible to gather there at all. For now, in the deserted living room, it was just himself and Em.

His first thought was to palm the urn like a football and run with it. To cradle it against his chest and dash toward some goal in the distance, some place where he'd have her, or what was left of her physical body, all to himself.

He lifted the urn in his two big hands, surprised at its weight, its heft. In the burnished silver his reflection wavered, indistinct. It took every ounce of moral strength he possessed to set her down, to turn away, to leave her where she had asked to be in the end, within the bosom of her family.

"Good-bye, old girl," he said.

He went to the door, stood for a moment in the doorway, stuck between the coffee table and the rest of his life. The old tomato-red pickup waited at the curb at the end of the walk, through the broken gate, a dozen steps, no more than that, but his strength had left him. He had no will to move on.

"Isn't that just like a man?"

He spun around. "What?"

"To take right off without a backward glance. Fickle, that's what I'd call it." She laughed, that deep, merry chuckle completely her own.

He turned and looked in the other direction, even though he knew he wouldn't find her there.

"Did you really think it was over between us? That it could ever be over between us?"

"No! Em! I—" He threw up his hands in protest, scanned the sky as if her voice were coming from there.

"I thought you were smart. That you had imagination. And now look at you."

"I do. I do have imagination. You know that." He realized that he was whispering, hissing his answers, no longer bold. He cared what Emily's gentle friends would think should they look out the window and see him talking to himself there on the stoop.

"Oh, don't worry about them," she said. "They'll all have their chance soon enough." But he hurried to his truck just the same and closed himself inside.

"What on earth are you mooning about, Jeronimo?" said Emily's voice. "I'm right here."

"But I can't see you," he wailed.

"Of course you can't see me. What did you expect?"

He laid his forehead against the steering wheel and closed his eyes. "Oh, Em," he moaned, "am I losing my mind? Have I finally gone round the bend?"

She said nothing for several seconds as his heart pounded. It had always been the great fear of his life, that he would lose his rational processes, lose hold of his mind. "Could be," she said at last. "That's up to you to decide."

He raised his head, slapped the wheel with the palm of his hand. "Ha! I can choose to go crazy, is that it? Or not. Emily, you're a real corker, you know that? Anybody ever tell you that?"

"As a matter of fact, yes. I thanked her."

"Well, I choose not to be crazy. How's that?"

"It's a start," she said.

He laughed. He cranked the engine, drove away from 467 Laguna, and joined the flow of tourist traffic on State Street. With his windows rolled down, he passed the art museum and then the café where, in his haste to grab the check, he'd turned the table over. "If I haven't lost my mind," he said after a while, "how is it that I can talk to you? How do you explain that?"

"Do I have to explain everything? You said you had imagination."

"Oh, *right*," he scoffed. "Imagination. Mind games. I know what you're up to. Don't think I don't."

She was quiet, probably waiting to hear what he'd say next.

"You're talking . . . ha! You're talking life after death, right? Spooks and spirits. Emily Parsons. Emily *Wardlaw* Parsons. You know I'm not a religious man. Never have been. No rational person believes that life-after-death stuff. Wishful thinking, that's all it is. Fantasy."

"Hmm," she said.

"Isn't it? Well, isn't it?"

"As I've said, it's all up to you." He heard her yawn. "I just hope we don't have to spend the rest of your life arguing about it."

The old pickup continued down State Street toward the freeway going north to San Francisco, past the wharf where flags fluttered and fifty-foot palm trees swayed and people went sailing on with their lives as if they were certain to go on forever. They passed in cars and on bicycles, on skateboards or on foot. Some of them turned when they heard the old man in the tomato-red pickup truck talking to himself. Some laughed, some shook their heads. And there were those who might have thought he was just another crazy soul, beating his steering wheel, waving his arms, laughing at nothing but the voices in his mind. But they'd have been wrong.